Showdown in Jeopardy

In the depths of a winter's night, a train is sent off its tracks near Cutler's Pass and raided for the $80,000 gold shipment it's carrying. Just after midnight, five years later in the town of Jeopardy, ex-Bostonian Clyde Pascoe is puzzling over the anonymous arrival of a newspaper cutting. Minutes later, he is shot and killed by an unknown assassin.

Sheriff Cyrus Yapp and local newspaper editor, Will Bullard, are soon making the connection between Pascoe's death and the five-year-old train raid and wondering if newcomer to Jeopardy, Luke Frey, is mixed up in the murders that suddenly occur in this once peaceful town. Luke, however, is more interested in discovering the identity of the train's mysterious fifth raider. But why?

Showdown in Jeopardy

John Davage

A Black Horse Western

ROBERT HALE · LONDON

ISBN 978-0-7090-9304-6

Robert Hale Limited
Clerkenwell House
Clerkenwell Green
London EC1R 0HT

www.halebooks.com

Typeset by
Derek Doyle & Associates, Shaw Heath
Printed and bound in Great Britain by
CPI Antony Rowe, Chippenham and Eastbourne

PROLOGUE

Smoke curled up into the frosty, star-speckled night sky and streamed behind the shining locomotive. The rails under its wheels sparked and shimmered as its lamps poured out a ribbon of light into the blackness ahead. Flakes of snow fluttered in the icy wind and there was a bite in the wintry air.

The locomotive had picked up speed in the last few miles, much to the satisfaction of Gabe Turner, its driver. Its firebox doors were open and the reflection of the flames glowed brightly on the faces of Gabe and Lew Traten, his young fireman.

Although neither man had an inkling of what was about to happen, both were conscious of the $80,000 gold shipment secured in the caboose. And both would be a lot happier when they reached Cannersville, their destination and were rid of it.

Gabe had been driving locomotives like this one for nigh on ten years, but never had he felt so nervous. It was if he had a presentiment of trouble ahead.

'Damn fool thinkin'!' he chided himself.

The Cannersville train consisted of a locomotive and tender, a baggage car, two passenger coaches and the caboose. The coaches were two-thirds full, most of the passengers dozing or reading. An armed guard was with the brakeman in the caboose. Both men were relaxing over a game of cards.

A mile ahead, around a bend at Cutler's Pass, a huge rock, a pile of smaller rocks, fence rails and the trunk of a large tree were stacked in a heap and lay across the track.

A hundred yards further along, in the bushes at the top of the sloping scorched grass of the embankment, four mounted and neckerchief-masked figures waited. A fifth figure, unmasked but just a silhouette in the moonlight, sat astride a horse on a knoll some distance from the others, surveying the scene.

The rhythmic rumble of the rails swelled as the train neared, and the riders on the embankment straightened up on their horses and loosened the .45s in their holsters in readiness.

The locomotive rattled round the bend without slowing.

'Sweet Jesus!'

Gabe gave out a stream of oaths when he saw what was ahead of them. Lew, eyes wide with terror, was struck dumb.

Gabe went for the brake, but already it was too late. The loco's cowcatcher ploughed into the barrier, scattering some of the fence rails and smaller rocks but buckling under the impact when it hit the large rock and tree trunk. The loco jack-knifed, hurtled off the rails, lurched sideways, and rolled into the embankment pulling its carriages after it. Gabe and Lew were thrown from the cab, and both men were crushed to death as the locomotive landed on top of them.

The raiders had pinpointed the position of the train's final resting place with uncanny accuracy, and were within twenty yards of the stricken caboose, now half on its side. Its roof, now almost vertical to the embankment, had been split open by the impact of the crash.

'Let's go!' one of the men shouted.

The raiders went directly to the caboose. Three dropped down through the roof whilst the other tended their horses. Inside, the three were confronted with a stunned brakeman and a security guard reaching for his gun. One of the raiders turned and shot the latter through the head. Then, for good measure, turned again and shot the brakeman.

He laughed out loud. 'Like takin' candy from a baby!' he shouted.

Another, with an accent that revealed his Bostonian upbringing, said coldly, 'You didn't have to do that. We could have knocked them out.'

The other raider pulled down his mask and spat at the Bostonian's feet. 'Don't tell me what to do, Adams!'

'Quit talkin', Nate!' a third raider shouted. 'Let's get what we came for.'

Further forward, in one of the two passenger coaches which hung at crazy angles over the embankment, the conductor, a middle-aged man greying at his temples, stumbled over prone and screaming passengers. Blood poured down one side of his face where he had been thrown against a window which had disintegrated instantly.

'Stay calm!' he pleaded above the noise of the screams. 'Stay calm and we'll get you out somehow.'

As he spoke, he saw that some people had been thrown *through* windows and lay sprawled on the blackened grass. It was immediately clear to the conductor that several were dead.

A young woman was crouched over the twisted form of a small child. She was weeping uncontrollably.

The conductor scrunched his way across splintered wood and glass towards the hole where, minutes before, a window had been. Ignoring the cuts he sustained to his hands in the process, he pulled himself out on to the embankment.

The three masked riders emerged from the caboose and clambered on to their horses. Each carried conspicuously bulging saddlebags as they and the fourth raider steered their mounts between the scattering of injured or dead bodies.

'Why don't we stop and see what we can get from these folk?' the fourth raider said.

'That's not the plan,' said the man with the Bostonian accent, an edge to his voice. 'And we stick to the plan!'

The rider who had shot the guard and the brakeman looked towards the young woman with the child – at the precise moment that she glanced up at him. His eyes narrowed above his neckerchief mask and he let out a whoop of delight.

'Well, I'm gonna get me a keepsake!' he yelled.

And ignoring the protests of two of his three compatriots, he stooped, threw an arm round the woman's waist and scooped her up alongside him like a sack of corn. The woman screamed, her arms outstretched towards her child, eyes wide with horror.

Moments later all four riders and the struggling

woman disappeared over the top of the embankment. Then, when it was clear they'd got clean away, the rider who had been waiting on the hillock watching the proceedings, also receded into the night.

CHAPTER ONE

Clyde Pascoe, sat at his desk in the real estate office in Jeopardy's Main Street. He was a tall, spare man, in his forties and dressed entirely in black. His eyes were cold with black pupils, his mouth a crooked knife-slash beneath a sweeping blonde moustache.

An oil lamp threw shadows into corners of the room and across Clyde's perplexed face. He was staring at a newspaper cutting, lost in thought and with a deep frown under his thatch of grey-blonde hair.

After several minutes he went to throw it into the wastebasket by his chair, then changed his mind. Instead he took a paste pot from a shelf above his desk and carefully stuck the cutting to the underside of a desk drawer. Satisfied, he pushed the drawer back into place.

11

'But I need to discover who sent it,' he muttered to himself. 'I need to know what *they* know, if I'm to sleep easy from now on.'

It was after midnight but, outside, Jeopardy's Main Street was far from quiet. Clyde leaned back in his swivel chair, closed his eyes, and tried to shut out the sound of the Circle Y cowhands who were carousing outside the Scarlet Slipper saloon, taking pot shots at the sign and yelling encouragement to one another.

He tried to think. Somebody had pushed the newspaper cutting under his office door sometime that afternoon. Somebody who wanted to frighten him? If that was the case, they had certainly succeeded. For five years, Clyde Pascoe had felt safe. Now he felt as if he had suddenly stepped on a deadly patch of quicksand.

So deep in thought was he that he did not hear the door of his office open quietly behind him. He did not see the other man's shadow move across the floor. And when, at last, he looked up, it was too late.

The report from the killer's .45 Peacemaker seemed to merge with the explosions in the street. The slug penetrated Clyde's head, passed through, and lodged itself in the wall behind the shelf beyond. He was dead before his upper torso hit the desk with a crash.

The killer stared at the dead man for a moment,

then began emptying the desk drawers and sweeping objects from the shelves in a desperate search for something. But after several minutes, he had satisfied himself that Pascoe had nothing that would prove a danger to him.

'It was all talk,' he muttered under his breath. 'So much for his "I've got written proof". He couldn't have proved a damn thing! Why'n hell didn't I call his bluff?'

He gave a last cursory look around the room then, after checking the street outside, left as silently as he had arrived.

CHAPTER TWO

At nine-thirty the next morning, three men stood silently looking at the body of Clyde Pascoe. One was the sheriff of Jeopardy, Cyrus Yapp. His face was expressionless. During his fifty-odd years he had seen many a dead man with half their head blown away.

Next to him stood his young deputy, Chet Smith, whose features were the colour of cold porridge. He was having trouble keeping down the ham and eggs he'd eaten at Carrie's café just half an hour earlier.

The third man was Will Bullard, editor of Jeopardy's weekly *Clarion* newspaper. A little man, skinny with thinning hair which he combed over his otherwise bald pate, and a sparse greying beard. He sucked on an empty cherrywood pipe and his expression was one of intense curiosity, as befitting a newspaperman with the makings of a story in front of him.

14

'What d'you reckon, Cyrus?' he asked.

Cyrus sniffed and stuck his thumbs in his waist-coat. There was a gap between this and his belt, over which his stomach hung.

'Been dead a few hours, looks like,' he said. 'Doc McReedy might have a better idea when he gets here.'

'Doc's on his way,' Chet confirmed. 'I stopped off on the way here. He was havin' his breakfast, but he said he'll be here directly.'

He was avoiding looking at the corpse and was staring at the floor. Books and files which had been on the shelves, plus the contents of the desk drawers, lay scattered across the floorboards.

'Whoever killed him was mighty anxious to find somethin',' Cyrus said. 'Money, maybe. Wonder if they did?'

'Or maybe to *make it look as though* they were searching for something,' Will said, shrewdly. He was never one to take things at face value.

Chet used his foot to move some of the papers around. After a moment, he turned over one of the drawers with the toe of his boot.

'Hey, there's somethin' stuck to the bottom of this,' he said suddenly, and he stooped down and picked up the drawer.

'Give it here,' Cyrus told him.

The sheriff carefully peeled off the newspaper cutting. It was brown and slightly brittle with age but it came off easily. He placed it on the desk a few inches from the dead man's splayed fingers, and the three men leaned forward to read the headline and opening sentence.

$80,000 GOLD SHIPMENT ROBBERY!
Fifteen people died and thirty more were injured in daring train robbery at Cutler's Pass yesterday morning. . . .'

Cyrus stopped reading to check the date at the top of the paper. 'This cuttin's five years old,' he said.

'Maybe it is,' Will said, after a moment. 'But it's not been on the bottom of that drawer for five years.'

'Eh?' Cyrus said.

'Look at the colour of that paste,' Will said. '*It's new*. If you ask me, Pascoe only stuck the cutting there recently.'

Cyrus peered at the bottom of the drawer and touched it with his fingertips. 'Sonofabitch! You're right, Will. It's barely dry.'

'Reckon this is what Pascoe's killer was lookin' for?' Chet asked. 'The drawer was right side up on the floor, so he could've missed it.'

Will shrugged. 'Maybe.'

16

He and Cyrus read through the rest of the newspaper cutting.

'What's it say?' Chet asked. Reading wasn't something he'd mastered to any degree. The headline had been as much as he could manage.

'Seems they blocked the railway track and sent the train down an embankment at Cutler's Pass. That's more'n four hundred miles north of here,' Cyrus told him. 'Then they broke into the caboose and shot the guard and brakeman. Eye witnesses reckon there were four raiders.'

Will was looking at the cutting more closely. 'Seems to me, this is only *part* of the report,' he said. 'Looks like somebody's snipped off the end of it.'

At that moment, a wiry-haired, black-suited imitation of a buzzard entered the realty office, clutching a brown leather bag. 'What'n hell's happened here?' Doc McReedy demanded.

He stooped across the desk and peered at the dead man. 'Jeez, he's been shot through the head!'

'Tell us something we don't know, Doc,' Will said.

'Like how long he's been dead?' Cyrus added.

Doc McReedy took several minutes to sniff and prod the corpse before announcing, 'Damn long time! Mebbe eight, ten hours.'

'That puts it around midnight last night.' Will stroked his sparse whiskers. 'How come nobody

17

heard the shot?'

'With all the ruckus the Circle Y boys were kickin' up at the Scarlet Slipper and in the street outside, t'ain't that surprisin',' Cyrus said.

'Shootin' up half the street, takin' pot shots at the sign outside the saloon,' Chet agreed. 'Wanda came out screamin' and yellin' at 'em fit to bust! Sign's peppered with holes this mornin'.'

'Got four of 'em sleepin' it off in my cells.' Cyrus looked back at the body. 'Best get Abel to take care of him,' he said, referring to the local undertaker. 'Nothin' you can do for him, Doc.'

Will picked up the newspaper cutting. 'Mind if I borrow this?' he asked Cyrus. 'Maybe I can get hold of the rest of the report. My guess is it's from the *Stanfield Gazette* if it's the Cutler's Pass I'm thinking of, which is only forty or so miles from the town of Stanfield. Reckon I'll wire the editor there and see if he's got a back copy of the newspaper. Might be interesting to see what else it's got to say.'

'Go ahead,' Cyrus said. 'But keep it to yourself for the time bein'. Meantime, Chet an' I had better start askin' around. See if anybody knows or heard anythin'. He sighed. 'Never did like this Pascoe fellah. Always knew he'd cause me a headache one of these days.'

CHAPTER THREE

The news of Clyde Pascoe's murder travelled fast. Within an hour, most of the townsfolk knew of it and were speculating about the possible identity of the killer. Two young men in particular were exchanging views on the subject.

The Hurley twins, Nate and Mitch, were sitting at a corner table in the Scarlet Slipper saloon, a near-empty bottle of gut-rot whiskey and a glass in front of one of them. The saloon was only quarter full, but was still filled with a drifting haze of smoke and the stale smell of the previous night's sweaty bodies and bad breath. A barkeep was wiping glasses and talking to two men sitting astride stools at the bar. A poker game was in progress at one end of the room, and a weary-looking bargirl sat at the foot of the stairs that led to the rooms above the bar. None of these people was taking any interest in the two young men talking earnestly at a corner table.

The twins were aged twenty, but Mitch was the older by twenty-nine minutes as he frequently reminded his brother. They had similar square-cut features, marked by numerous fist-fights and bar room brawls. And Nate had scar which stretched from his chin to his left eye, a permanent reminder of a knife fight with a drunk when he'd been just fifteen years old. The drunk had come off worse, losing an ear.

They glanced around from time to time making certain their conversation wasn't being overheard.

'Couldn't have had anythin' to do with you-know-what, could it?' Nate said.

'Can't see how,' his brother replied. 'Ain't likely Pascoe would have spoken of it.'

'Hope you're right,' Nate said.

'An' nobody in Jeopardy knows about it, as far as I know,' Mitch went on. 'An' even if'n they do, they ain't likely to make the connection with Pascoe or his murder.'

Nate nodded slowly. 'Reckon so.' His mood brightened as he saw one of the saloon girls leaning over a banister at the top of the stairs. She had chestnut-coloured hair and wore a figure-hugging green dress which emphasized the size of her breasts and the depth of her cleavage.

Nate felt a stirring in his loins. 'Reckon I'll pay Hettie a visit for a spell,' he said, and gulped down the rest of his whiskey. 'See you later, brother.'

Mitch sighed and watched him stagger up the stairs towards the grinning Hettie. Sometimes he worried about Nate. Not because of his brother's womanizing. Mitch was no slouch in that department himself, and he was very familiar with Hettie's charms between the sheets. No, he was more concerned about Nate's loose tongue after he'd had a few drinks. And just lately Nate's drinking had begun progressively earlier in the day.

After a few minutes, Mitch eased himself from his chair and headed for the batwing doors and the street. As he did so, he looked across towards the bar and tipped his hat to the woman standing next to the barkeep.

Wanda Decker, owner of the Scarlet Slipper, nodded in acknowledgement and watched him leave. Nate's visit to Hettie hadn't escaped her notice, either. Earlier, she had watched the powwow between the two brothers and had accurately guessed its subject – Clyde Pascoe's murder. It was something she'd been cogitating about herself.

With a certain amount of unease.

CHAPTER FOUR

Luke Frey heard about the real estate agent's killing whilst he was tucking into a late breakfast in Carrie's café. Late because he'd spent the previous hour washing the dishes of the earlier diners. It was his way of contributing towards his rent.

Carrie herself imparted the information as she poured him a third mug of coffee.

'Don't suppose you knew Clyde Pascoe, you being a relative newcomer to the town, Luke,' she said.

'Nope,' Luke agreed. 'Seen him playin' poker in the Scarlet Slipper a few times, but that's all. He looked to be a man who liked to gamble, and he seemed to win more often than he lost. Maybe his killer was a sorc loser.'

He studied Carrie's plump but pleasing features and silently congratulated himself on choosing to rent the room above the café rather than stay at the hotel across the street when he'd arrived in town ten days ago.

Sensing his scrutiny, she coloured a little and smiled at the long, lanky figure of her newest tenant. 'Luke Frey, stop giving me the once-over, you're making me blush.' She slopped coffee over the side of his mug. 'There! Now look what you made me do!'

He smiled. 'Excuse me, ma'am.'

She slapped the back of his hand before moving away, chuckling to herself.

Luke sipped his coffee thoughtfully. He hadn't been strictly honest with Carrie. All right, he had only spoken half a dozen words to Clyde Pascoe, but he reckoned he knew something about the man that most folk in town didn't.

He finished his coffee and made his way out into the street. The town was a huddle of small buildings strung out along Main Street. Two saloons, livery, mercantile, feed store, telegraph office, bank and sheriff's office. And twenty yards along the boardwalk from Carrie's café was Gus Tute's Barber Shop.

Luke decided that his greying locks could do with a trim. For a man of thirty-three, he had more than his fair share of grey hairs. The cause of them rarely left his thoughts and frequently gave him nightmares, but he'd not shared the secrets of his past with anyone in town, nor his real reasons for being in Jeopardy, although he was aware that folk had begun speculating about them behind his back.

'Howdy, Mr Frey,' Gus greeted him. 'Heard about the murder?' He was lathering the chin of his other customer with shaving soap.

'Yeah, I heard,' Luke replied, settling himself on the bench next to the window to wait his turn in the barber's chair.

'I was tellin' the mayor here,' Gus went on, 'young Chet Smith says Pascoe's office was in a mess – drawers emptied, papers everywhere. Could've been robbery was behind the killin' if'n Pascoe kept money there.'

'Then he was a fool,' the man in the chair said, as Gus began to wield a razor an inch from his chin. 'Should've put it in my bank where it would've been safe.'

Luke picked up a copy of the previous week's *Clarion* and began leafing through it. But his mind was elsewhere. Could there be an entirely different motive behind Pascoe's killing? Maybe linked to a certain newspaper cutting? A report of a five-year-old train robbery? A cutting which Luke had slipped under the door of Pascoe's office the previous afternoon?

Gus finished shaving the banker, who eased his

24

portly form from the barber's chair. He was dressed in a white alpaca suit which was stained with tobacco juice.

He stared at Luke for several seconds before coming forward with a chubby hand outstretched.

'We haven't met,' he said. 'George Drummond's the name. I run Jeopardy's one and only bank. I was out of town on business when you arrived. Only got back from Tucson a couple of days ago.'

Luke stood and shook the other man's hand. 'Howdy. I'm Luke Frey.' His eyes narrowed. 'Have we met someplace before? You look kinda familiar.'

Drummond's face coloured. 'Don't reckon we have.' He turned away quickly, dropped a coin into Gus's hand, then took his broad-brimmed planter's hat from the peg by the door. 'So long, Gus,' he said. 'Good day to you, Mr Frey.'

Luke watched him go before sitting himself in the barber's chair. 'Dresses more like a Mississippi gambler than a banker,' he observed.

Gus laughed. 'Sure does. Kinda flamboyant, is our mister mayor. Now, what'll it be? Shave, haircut or both?'

'Guess I'll have both,' Luke said. 'How long has Drummond lived in Jeopardy?'

Gus began mixing a fresh bowl of shaving soap. He thought for a moment. 'Reckon nigh on five years now,' he said.

'Is that right?' Luke said.

There it was again. The magic number . . . five. Five men. Five years.

'Where'd he come *from*?'

'Couldn't say,' Gus answered. 'Don't know as anybody knows. Just showed up, he and his wife. She's ten years younger'n him. No more'n thirty, if she's a day. Strikin' lookin' woman, Harmony, with a sharp tongue. Jeopardy didn't have a bank, as such, when they arrived. Afore then you kept your money under the bed or buried it in your yard.'

'Gotta have money to set up a bank,' Luke said. 'Wonder where Drummond got his from?'

'Couldn't say,' Gus said. 'Anyways, within a year, he was town mayor and nigh on runnin' the town. Shows what money can do.'

'Interestin',' Luke observed.

'You plannin' on settlin' in Jeopardy, Mr Frey?'

'The name's Luke, Gus,' Luke told him. 'An' I ain't made my mind up about stayin'. Maybe.'

'Reckon you'd be mighty comfortable at Widow Mitford's place.' He gave Luke a broad wink. 'Nice woman, Carrie.'

'Yeah, I'm comfortable,' Luke said.

'You ever been married?'

A familiar knot formed in Luke's gut. 'Yeah, I was

26

married once,' he said, quietly.

Something about the tone of his voice forestalled further questions from Gus, who began lathering Luke's face with more than his usual concentration.

Luke returned his attention to the *Clarion*.

CHAPTER FIVE

When George Drummond left the barbershop, he did not head for the bank but made a beeline for the Scarlet Slipper. Beads of cold sweat clung to his brow and his hands were shaking.

Thoughts buzzed around his head like angry hornets: *Who in hell was this Frey character? What was he doing in Jeopardy? And how come he thought he knew me?*

The barkeep, seeing the agitated look on the mayor's face, opened a fresh bottle of rye in readiness.

'You OK, Mr Drummond?' he enquired.

'What? Oh, sure, Eddie.' George adjusted his features to give the appearance of insouciance as the barkeep poured his drink. 'Sure, I'm just fine.'

He took his glass and the bottle to a table, not wanting the distraction of a conversation. He needed to think.

But he wasn't alone for long. Wanda Decker emerged from her office at the back of the bar and strolled across to join him. Her intentions were purely sociable – until she saw the worried expression on the mayor's face.

'You look as though you've had a shock, George,' she said, sliding her ample behind on to a chair opposite him.

George gave a nervous smile. 'No, no,' he protested. 'Just thinking.'

'How's that young wife of yours? Puttin' a sparkle in your eyes? Givin' you plenty of activity between the sheets, eh?'

'Oh, she sure does!'

George affected a worldly laugh – which didn't fool Wanda for one second. She had seen him creeping in the back entrance of the Scarlet Slipper often enough, heading for the pleasures provided by one of her girls. Which meant he wasn't getting similar delights at home.

She watched him with a calculating eye for several seconds, then said, 'You've got somethin' on your mind, George.' It wasn't a question.

George poured himself another drink, downed it in one noisy gulp.

'What d'you know about this Frey fellah?' he said.

Wanda raised her eyebrows. 'Luke Frey? Not

much. Quiet sorta critter. He's rentin' a room above Carrie Mitford's café, an' helpin' out waitin' tables an' doin' dishes. Only been in town a week or so.'

'Where's he from?'

Wanda shrugged. 'He ain't said. Like I told you, he ain't talkative. Why? Somethin' tuggin' at your tail, George?'

'No reason,' George said. 'I was just curious, that's all.'

Wanda wasn't fooled. There was more to George's question than mere curiosity, she was sure, but she decided to let it lie – for the moment.

A red-faced, somewhat dishevelled Nate Hurley descended the stairs and exited from the saloon. He had the satiated look of a man who has had his bodily needs well and truly catered for.

A moment later, Hettie appeared on the landing and peered down into the bar, as if looking for another potential customer. Her eyes alighted on George and she gave him a broad grin and winked.

'Hey there, George!' she called. 'You comin' to see me?'

George 'Hrrrmphed!' and got up to leave, his face red, his eyes avoiding those of the saloon girl.

Wanda hid a smile and said, 'See you soon, George. If I discover anythin' else about Luke Frey, I'll let you know.'

'What? Oh, yeah,' he said, making for the door. 'It's not important, but, er, thanks.'

Once outside, he headed towards the refuge of his bank.

CHAPTER SIX

Chet Smith spent most of the day asking folk if they'd seen or heard anything that might give him and Cyrus some clue to Clyde Pascoe's killing. By mid-afternoon, the time he got to the Scarlet Slipper, his feet were aching and he was in need of several beers, and maybe some congenial female company.

The barkeep was attending to two cowpokes, so it was Wanda who served Chet with his glass of beer.

'Tough mornin', Chet?' she enquired.

'Yeah,' he replied. 'Waste of time, too. Nobody knows nothin'.'

'About Clyde Pascoe's killin'? Well, that ain't surprisin',' Wanda said. 'Folks sayin' his killer was somebody after money.'

'That's what the sheriff reckons, too,' Chet said. 'Pascoe was here last night, wasn't he? Early, I mean.

Afore the Circle Y boys started causin' a ruckus.'

Wanda nodded. 'Playin' poker with Mitch an' Nate Hurley, an' later with Pete Buss and Carl Darby. An' knowin' Clyde, he probably won money off all of 'em.'

'Yeah, he did,' Chet said. 'Pete at the mercantile and Carl at the livery both admitted that much. So he prob'ly took home a fistful of cash.'

'An' one or two of the Circle Y boys could've noticed that,' Wanda said, thoughtfully.

'An', later on, when some of their pals were divertin' attention shootin' up the place, they went to collect!' Chet's face lit up. 'Hey it could've been like that!'

'Yeah,' Wanda said. She looked as if she wanted to believe it, but wasn't entirely convinced. 'Yeah, maybe.'

Chet avoided her eye. 'Er . . . Hettie free?'

Wanda laughed. 'Reckon she is. Why, you in need of some . . . recreation?'

Chet grinned. 'Guess I am,' he said.

'Well, you know which is her room,' Wanda said. 'Get your hide up there double quick, afore someone else gets the same idea.'

'Yeah, guess I will,' Chet said, swallowing the last of his beer.

33

George Drummond strode into the bank, ignoring the glances of the teller at the counter and his chief clerk at his roll-top desk. George pushed through the swinging gate of the railing and went on to his office at the back of the bank.

He sat down at his own desk and, ignoring the pile of paperwork requiring his attention, searched his memory for some clue as to where Luke Frey might have seen him. Only one place he could think of – and that was more than a hundred miles from here. He sure as hell hoped it wasn't there. But where else could it have been? Before coming to Jeopardy, George had spent more than ten years in that little one-horse town, and hated every minute of it.

Mind you, it hadn't been George *Drummond* who had lived there; that was a name he and Harmony had adopted on their arrival in Jeopardy. First name he'd thought of, as it happened. And that had been near-on five years ago.

And it had been a good five years, damn it! Setting up the bank, winning enough local support to get himself appointed mayor of the town. OK, maybe that had involved calling in a few favours and granting a couple of interest-free loans, but what the heck! Now he was a man of influence, somebody folks respected.

If he *had* made a mistake, it was probably marrying

Harmony. He hadn't realized what a little witch she was when she'd beguiled him with her shapely bosom and her pert little ass. Daughter of the one-horse town's church minister, she'd been soft-spoken and demure in her manner, lowering her cornflower-blue eyes whenever he'd smiled at her across the choir stalls. But little miss butter-wouldn't-melt had turned into a fire-breathing hell-cat once he'd put a ring on her finger!

Maybe her pa – a widower of many years – had been relieved to be rid of his sharp-tongued, short-tempered offspring, even if, at the time, George had been nothing more than a lowly bank clerk with very few prospects. Maybe her pa had thought that, at twenty-three, Harmony was in danger of becoming a life-long spinster and resident in his home, which had probably had something to do with the alacrity with which he'd given his blessing to George's pro-posal of marriage.

Harmony.

Ha! If ever there'd been a woman misnamed it was George's wife. Hadn't it been her screeching, nagging voice that had finally brow-beaten him into finding a way to get them out of that one-horse town and on their way to prosperity?

And he had!

George – a fat, balding, insignificant little bank

clerk, undervalued by his employers and despised by his new wife – had devised a plan that had shocked even Harmony by its audacity.

And, as a result, for near on five years they had lived a comfortable, well-heeled existence. Until now, when everything seemed threatened to go to hell in a handcart!

CHAPTER SEVEN

Chet lay beside Hettie with a gratified smile on his face. Heck, she sure knew how to make a man forget a frustrating, wearisome morning! A morning of questions without any useful answers. A tedious, irksome exercise which had produced nothing but a couple of sore feet and an aching head.

But Hettie had provided the remedy in her inimitable way, and now he was feeling mellow enough to purr like a contented cat.

She was stroking the side of his face and smiling down at him, her bare breasts brushing his chest. 'That better, honey?' she cooed.

'You know damn well it is,' he told her. 'Jeez, Hettie, when you start up with that—'

She pressed her fingers on his lips. 'Shh!' she

said, with that low, guttural laugh which turned a fellah's insides to jelly. 'I just happen to know what you like.'

'You sure do!' he said. 'My mornin' may have started grim, thanks to Mr Pascoe, but it's finishin' on a high!'

She looked quizzically at him. 'Clyde Pascoe killed for money, was he?'

'Seems like it. Although there was one strange thing.'

'What was that?'

'A newspaper cuttin', stuck to the bottom of one of his desk drawers.'

Hettie frowned, cupping her chin in her hand. 'A cuttin' about what?'

Chet explained about the five-year-old train robbery. But he was too busy staring at her naked bosom to see her expression slowly change from simple curiosity to a more calculating look.

'So what's Cyrus sayin' about it?' she asked, when Chet had finished.

Chet shrugged. 'You know Cyrus. Only looks for the obvious, so he reckons Pascoe was killed for his cash. But Will Bullard was more interested in the train robbery angle. Fact, he's gonna see what he can find out from the editor of the newspaper it came from.'

'Is he now,' Hettie said quietly, more to herself than to Chet.

He looked at her questioningly. 'What?' he said. 'You know somethin' I don't?'

'Mm? No, of course I don't.' She began to run her fingers along the inside of his thigh to divert his attention and get his mind on other things.

'Jeez, Hettie!' he moaned.

It was having the desired effect. Which was good, because she didn't want to reveal what *she* knew about the Cutler's Pass train robbery. Not to Chet, anyway.

An hour later, Hettie found Mitch having lunch in Carrie Mitford's eating house. The half-dozen other diners looked up in surprise when she breezed through the door and seated herself down opposite Mitch. He was mopping up gravy with a thick chunk of bread from his otherwise empty plate and looked surprised to see her.

Carrie Mitford looked equally surprised, and not particularly pleased by the appearance of the saloon girl. She strode across, a coffee pot in her hand.

'You wantin' somethin', Hettie,' Carrie asked.

'Just wantin' to talk with Mitch here,' Hettie replied. 'That OK, Mizz Mitford?'

'This ain't a meetin' house, it's a café,' Carrie

39

reminded the girl.

'OK, pour me a cuppa coffee,' Hettie said. She dragged Mitch's mug towards her. 'He'll pay.'

Mitch nodded at Carrie. 'Go ahead,' he told her.

Carrie gave a sniff and slopped coffee into the mug before walking away. The other diners, all male, stared at Hettie with lascivious grins on their faces until she scowled at them and yelled, 'What'ya lookin' at?', whereupon they quickly lost interest.

'What's on your mind, Hettie,' Mitch asked, 'other than a free cuppa coffee?'

She sipped her coffee and leaned across the table. She lowered her voice. 'Chet Smith paid me a visit earlier,' she said. 'Let somethin' interestin' slip whilst I was keepin' him amused.'

'Oh, yeah? What was that?'

'About Clyde Pascoe's murder.'

'What about it?'

'Seems Clyde had a certain old newspaper cuttin' in his possession . . . about a train robbery at Culter's Pass, five years ago.' She smiled. 'Now, don't you find that interestin'?'

Mitch's eyes narrowed. 'Yeah, reckon I do.' He put a hand on her wrist, gripping it so tightly that she almost dropped the coffee mug. 'But you ain't sup-posed to know anythin' about that little episode with the train, if you remember, Hettie. That was somethin' Nate let slip when he was drunk an' was beddin' you. Pillow talk, right?'

Hettie nodded quickly, wincing with pain as Mitch's hold on her wrist stopped the flow of blood. 'Sure, Mitch!' she gasped. 'Sure!'

He released her arm. 'Good. Now listen, you ain't gonna say nothin' about this to Nate, got it?'

'Sure, Mitch,' Hettie said again.

'An' you sure as hell ain't gonna say anythin' to anybody else, are you?'

Hettie shook her head.

'Good,' he said. 'Anythin' else you wanna tell me?'

'No, that was it, Mitch. I just thought . . . well. . . .' She glanced across at Carrie Mitford, who appeared to be watching the two of them with interest. 'Guess I'll be goin',' she said. 'Just thought you oughta know about the newspaper—'

'Yeah, yeah, OK,' Mitch said. 'Now get out of here.'

He watched her leave.

Could she be relied on to keep her pretty mouth shut, or should he do something about it? He swore under his breath. It was all down to Nate and his loose tongue again!

But why was Pascoe keeping an old newspaper cutting about the train robbery? Damn fool thing to do, when you thought about it. Or maybe he hadn't

41

been keeping it all of five years. Maybe somebody had given it to him recently. Somebody who knew about the robbery and was blackmailing him.

Could it have something to do with his killing? Had there been a gunfight, with Clyde gunned down by a man with a faster draw? In which case, how much did the mystery man know about the train robbery? Did he know who else had been involved?

Suddenly, the meat pie Mitch had just finished eating seemed to be burning a hole in his gut.

Hettie hurried away from the café, rubbing her wrist and cursing the name of Mitch Hurley.

'I'm wishin' I'd kept quiet about what Chet told me now,' she thought. 'Mitch is one mean sono-fabitch!'

She'd thought she was doing Mitch a favour, but she should've known better. Mitch was cruel, and he despised women like her at the same time as needing their services.

Still, there was something Mitch *didn't* know; something Hettie hadn't told him the day she'd informed him that his brother had drunkenly boasted about a train robbery at Cutler's Pass.

She hadn't told Mitch that Nate had *also* mentioned the name of the gang's leader. *That* tidbit of information she'd kept to herself.

And now she was wondering if she could make use
of it . . . *profitably* . . . .

CHAPTER EIGHT

George had trouble concentrating on business at the bank that afternoon. He tried to push thoughts of Luke Frey, and what the newcomer to Jeopardy might know, from his mind. But it was no use, he couldn't stop himself brooding about it and breaking out into a cold sweat at the same time.

The more he thought about it, the more he became convinced that he *had* seen Frey before, and that it had been in that little one-horse town he and Harmony had left in such a hurry. And if that was right, it was bad news indeed.

He was gloomily silent throughout supper that evening. Not that he and Harmony talked to one another much at the best of times, having run out of meaningful conversation months ago. Even so,

George usually made something of an effort over a meal.

Harmony was quick to notice. She peered at him across the table, her beady blue eyes bright with inquisitiveness, her beaky nose twitching.

'What's wrong with you, George,' she said, in that high-pitched reedy voice that had begun to grate on George's nerves within weeks of their marriage. 'Your sour expression is enough to curdle milk and you haven't spoken two words in the last hour.'

George debated whether or not to tell her about Luke Frey, but in the end decided against it. For one thing, he didn't want her fretting, and for another he hadn't made up his mind what to do about it.

'It's nothing, my dear,' he said, pushing his half-eaten plate of mutton and potatoes away from him. 'Just bank business. I had a particularly trying afternoon.'

Harmony looked sceptical. 'Millie Walton said she saw you coming out of the Scarlet Slipper this morning. Why were you drinking so early in the day, George? A guilty conscience? Or perhaps it wasn't a *drink* you went in for. Perhaps you were looking for *company*.'

George started to protest, but she held up a hand to stop him.

'Oh, don't bother to deny it,' she snapped. 'I know

45

what you're like, and I couldn't care less, providing you're discreet about it. But I do care about you making a spectacle of yourself because it reflects badly on me.'

'It was nothing like that!' George blustered, shocked to learn that Harmony knew about his associations with the saloon girls, and astonished to know that she didn't care. 'I-I wasn't feeling well and I thought a whiskey might help.'

Harmony sniffed disbelievingly but elected to say nothing more. Instead, she went to the kitchen to make coffee, leaving George with a stupefied expression on his face and his head in a spin.

Later, he said, 'I have to go out. Got to see Carl Darby about town council business.'

'Really?' Harmony was reading a book and did not look up. 'I shan't wait up and I don't want to be disturbed. Please be good enough to sleep on the couch in your study when you decide to return.'

George left the house fuming. He had no intention of going to see the livery man. He needed some female consolation; someone to take his mind off his worries.

Hettie. . . .

Hettie tried to calm her nerves with a shot of whiskey from the bottle she kept in her room. Her hand was shaking as she held the glass and her nerves were ragged, but it was decided. She would confront the person tonight.

Think of the money, she told herself. With a thousand dollars she could get out of Jeopardy and start up her own little place of entertainment a hundred miles away. It was what she'd always dreamed of doing, ever since she'd run away from home at fourteen, weary of her father's regular whippings and her mother's constant complaining.

And a thousand dollars would be nothing to the gang's leader. How much had they taken from the train? $80,000? True, it was five years ago, but unlike Nate and Mitch Hurley, and even Clyde Pascoe, the person she was going to speak with tonight wouldn't have blown it all away on booze and gambling.

Pascoe . . . who was dead. . . .

What about that? Was his killer the same person she was going to confront shortly? No, that wouldn't make any sense. Why would the leader of the gang kill one of its members, and after all this time? Also, there was the newspaper cutting Chet Smith had told her about. How did that fit in?

It was too much for Hettie. Her head started to ache whenever she tried to unravel complicated situations. Keep it simple, she told herself. But be careful.

Yes, be careful. . . .

Two hours later, a fistful of greasy dollars stuffed down the front of her bodice, Hettie's body lay in the alleyway at the back of the Scarlet Slipper, the back of her head a bloodied mess, her dead eyes staring into a starless sky.

Earlier, she had been reflecting on how easy it had been to extract half the thousand dollars from her target straight away, and get a promise of the other five hundred the next day. Once Hettie had told what she knew, there had been no argument, no threats necessary.

A simple business arrangement. A one-off payment for her silence. That's how it had been put to her, and she'd been more than happy to agree.

And after her benefactor had left her room, Hettie had celebrated with a large whiskey. With several large whiskeys, in fact. Resulting in her being in a drunken stupor when that same person had returned later, knowing full well what state Hettie would be in.

After that, it had been a simple matter to half-carry her intoxicated form down the back stairs and out into the alleyway at the side of the saloon. Even easier to use the butt of a .45 to beat her to death.

And now the killer stuffed a hand down the front

of Hettie's bodice and retrieved the money, before slipping away into the darkness.

At five minutes to midnight, George Drummond collapsed fully dressed on to the couch in his study. His heartbeat thumped in his ears and his breath came in short, painful gasps. There was blood on the cuffs of his pants and on his hand-tooled leather boots.

He closed his eyes, but knew that sleep was not something he could take refuge in tonight. And even if he did finally drop off, his dreams would quickly turn to nightmares after the events of the evening.

It was almost an hour later, his heartbeat finally back to its normal rhythm, that an idea came into his head. It was an audacious idea, but one that appealed to George a lot. He smiled. One that might well see off the tiresome Luke Frey.

After a minute, he made his way quietly up to the bedroom he sometimes shared with his wife – when he hadn't been relegated to the couch in his study. The loud snores coming from the bed indicated that Harmony was sleeping soundly.

Moving silently, he crossed the room to the small chest which stood next to Harmony's side of the bed, and opened the top drawer. It made a small sound, and Harmony stirred but did not wake up.

George removed a small lace handkerchief from

the drawer before shutting it again.

Minutes later, he was back in his study where, using the handkerchief, he began to wipe the blood from the toes of his boots.

CHAPTER NINE

Hettie's body was discovered early the following morning by the shirt-sleeved, bald-headed Eddie Ward, barkeep at the Scarlet Slipper. Eddie was depositing a crate of empty bottles in the alleyway when the crumpled shape of Hettie's emerald dress caught the corner of his eye. Minutes later, he was telling Wanda what he'd found, the emotion in his voice betraying the fact that Hettie had been a favourite of his.

'Get a hold of yourself, Eddie,' Wanda told him, putting an arm round his shoulders. 'Go fetch Cyrus. Meantime, I'll make sure nobody goes down the alleyway.' She shook her head. 'Sweet Jesus, poor Hettie! Who'n hell would want to harm her?'

Cyrus Yapp arrived on the scene with a sour look on his face. 'This is the second mornin' I've been dragged from my bed to view a corpse,' he grumbled. 'What in tarnation is happenin' to this town?'

He stooped to look at Hettie's bloodied head.

'Beaten to death, looks like,' he opined. 'One of your customer's get over-excited, Wanda? Get carried away with his—?'

'Out here in the alleyway?' Wanda cut in. 'Talk sense, Cyrus.'

'So what was she doin' out here?'

'Can't say,' Wanda answered. 'Thinkin' about it, I don't remember seein' her after about ten o'clock last night, but that ain't unusual. Hettie is – *was* – popular. Often had a string of fellah's waitin' their turn to go up to her room.' Wanda stared at the inert body. 'Guess she could've come out for a breath of air between times, down the back stairs into the alleyway. I guess somebody could've followed her down an'—' She sighed. 'Damn shame.'

They were silent for some moments, then Cyrus looked at Eddie. 'Better go tell Abe he's got another customer for one of his pine boxes,' he said.

'Reckon there's a connection between this and Clyde Pascoc's murder?' Eddie asked.

'How'n hell do I know!' Cyrus growled.

*

52

'It was a good question of Eddie's,' Cyrus admitted. '*Could* the same guy have killed both Hettie an' Pascoe?'

He and Will Bullard were sitting at a table in the Scarlet Slipper. Will had heard about Hettie from Abel Hartford, the undertaker, and had hurried to the alleyway, notebook at the ready. After Hettie's body had been removed, he and Cyrus had retired to the saloon. Wanda had brought a pot of strong coffee to the table, then gone to break the news to the other three bar girls.

'There's no obvious connection,' Will said. 'More likely to be some peeved or dissatisfied *hombre* who let his temper get the better of him. Mind you, that would be surprising seeing that Hettie always gave, uh' – he dropped his voice to a whisper – '*good value for money.*'

At that moment, the Hurley twins pushed their way through the batwings and marched into the saloon. They glanced round, then made a beeline for Cyrus's table.

'What's all this about Hettie?' Nate wanted to know. 'Is it true? She's dead?'

' 'Fraid so,' Cyrus said.

Nate swore. 'Best damn little whore I ever had, too! Like to get my hands on the bastard who did it!'

'Reckon you'd have to get in line,' Mitch said,

quietly. He frowned. 'Two murders in two days, Sheriff. What's goin' on? This here was always a quiet town. People who're mostly law-abidin'.'

Cyrus nodded. 'That's true.' He frowned. 'Ain't been no stranger passin' through, either.'

'One new face in town, though,' Wanda said, coming up behind the Hurley twins and joining in the conversation. She'd left three shocked and tearful saloon girls comforting one another.

'Who's that?' Mitch said.

'Luke Frey,' Wanda said. 'Been here about ten days now, an' he's kinda secretive, too. Reckon he's here on a mission? A *killin'* mission?'

'But why?' Will wanted to know. 'OK, he might've had some grudge against Clyde Pascoe that we don't know about, but *Hettie?* He don't look the sorta fellah to get all heated up and then lose his temper to the point where he'd kill a whore. And that's assuming he availed himself of her, um, services.'

'Even so, wouldn't do no harm to find out a bit more about him,' Mitch said. He glanced at Nate. 'Maybe hassle him a little.'

Nate grinned. 'Yeah.'

'Now don't go givin' me more trouble,' Cyrus warned them.

Will accompanied Cyrus back to the sheriff's office

where Chet was pacing up and down. He looked hot and agitated, and less than pleased to see Will.

'Got somethin' on your mind, young 'un?' Cyrus said, easing himself in to the chair behind his desk.

Will took a seat in a corner of the room. He, too, looked quizzically at Chet.

Chet wiped his face with his bandana. 'Listen, it might mean nothin', but I kinda let slip about the newspaper cuttin' to Hettie when I was, uh, talkin' with her.'

The two older men glanced at one another.

'*Talkin'* with her,' Cyrus repeated, a wry grin spreading across his face. 'Yeah, well sometimes a fella can get carried away when he gets *talkin'*.'

'But don't you see?' Chet hurried on. 'Now the newspaper cuttin's a kinda link between the two killin's.'

Will stuck his empty cherrywood pipe between his teeth and chewed on the stem. 'He's got a point, Cyrus. Kind of a coincidence that, when Hettie learns about the train robbery cutting – the same cutting Clyde Pascoe was hiding under his desk drawer – she gets herself killed.'

'She could have told somebody else about it,' Chet said, nodding.

'Or used it to try and extort hush money from someone,' Will said, warming to his idea.

'With what she knew!' Chet said.

'Yeah, but what *did* she know?' Cyrus said.

'Something about one or more of the train raiders?' Will said. 'Maybe somebody besides Chet had let something slip about a train robbery a while ago. Then when Chet told her the details of the Cutler's Pass robbery, from the newspaper cutting, she realized she knew something worth a pile of money.'

'Maybe the name of the gang leader!' Chet said, excitedly.

'Could be,' Cyrus said.

'Maybe he's been livin' here in Jeopardy!' Chet said. 'Reckon he'd want to keep Hettie's mouth shut – *permanent.*'

'So was Clyde Pascoe killed for the same reason?' Cyrus wanted to know. 'Did he suddenly discover the name of the gang leader an' try a touch of black-mail?'

'Could be,' Will said. 'I'm willing to bet he got that newspaper cutting the day he was killed.'

'But where'd he get it from?' Cyrus asked. 'That's what I wanna know.'

'I don't know, but it'd be mighty interesting to find out,' Will said.

'You heard anythin' from that newspaper editor in Stanfield yet?'

Will shook his head. 'I only wired him yesterday. Maybe I'll hear something later today, or tomorrow.'

CHAPTER TEN

Mitch and Nate watched Will Bullard come out of the sheriff's office and head towards the *Clarion*'s premises, a few steps along on the other side of the street. They were sitting sprawled in chairs on the boardwalk outside the Scarlet Slipper.

Most of the townsfolk couldn't be sure how the two of them got their money, but could make a shrewd guess. From time to time the twins would disappear from Jeopardy for several days. Then, soon after they returned, flush with cash again, there would be news of a stage hold-up, or a robbery in some nearby town. But the Hurley twins were not the sort you accused of anything unless you were prepared to back up your words with a gun, so folks turned a blind eye and said nothing. Including Sheriff Cyrus Yapp.

'Reckon Bullard is gettin' a bit too nosey for his own good,' Mitch said, as he built himself a smoke. 'Accordin' to Chet Smith, he's sent a wire to the *Stanfield Gazette* editor, askin' about the newspaper cuttin' Pascoe was keepin'.' After Hettie's death, he'd felt obliged to tell his brother what Hettie had told him.

'About Cutler's Pass?' Nate said.

Mitch nodded. 'He's got a notion that Pascoe might've been mixed up in the train robbery.'

'Yeah, well we *know* Pascoe was,' Nate said. 'But we don't want Bullard sniffin' out things about him, or about Stanfield.' He glanced at his brother. 'Want me to stop him?'

'Not yet,' Mitch said. 'Let's see what happens.'

At that moment, Luke Frey emerged from Carrie Mitford's eating house and headed towards the bank. Nate spotted him and yelled across the street.

'Hey, you! Frey!'

Luke stopped and looked up. He waited.

'Come over here!' Nate shouted.

Luke did not move for several seconds then, as if having come to a decision, strolled across to the boardwalk and waited on the street.

'Somethin' on your mind?' he asked Nate.

'Yeah, 's matter o' fact there is.' Nate eased himself from his chair and stepped down. 'Kinda close, ain't you? Don't say much, just keep your cards close to your chest.'

Luke smiled with his mouth but his eyes remained watchful. 'Mebbe,' he said.

'Kinda *unfriendly*, don'tcha think?'

Luke pushed his hands into the pockets of his jeans. 'What was it you wanted to know?'

'For a start, where d'you come from?'

'No place in particular,' Luke said. 'Just . . . around.'

'Plannin' on stayin' long?' Mitch asked, joining in from his seat on the boardwalk.

Luke glanced at him. 'Mebbe.'

'See what I mean?' Nate said, appealing to his brother. 'He's real cagey. Don't give nothin' away.' He turned and scowled at Luke. 'Me, I don't like a man who's that tight-lipped. Reckon he's got somethin' to hide. What d'you say?'

Luke stared, said nothing.

Nate moved forward so that his face was inches from Luke's. 'I asked you a question, mister. T'ain't polite, not answerin'.'

Luke gave a sigh and started to turn away. Nate grabbed his shoulder, turning him back. He swung his fist, driving it into Luke's stomach. Luke doubled up and staggered back but managed to dodge Nate's follow-through, aimed at his head. He steadied himself, moved forward and swung with his right fist, hitting Nate hard on the chin. The other man swayed for a moment, then lashed out with his boot, catching Luke on the thigh. Luke grabbed the boot and pushed.

Nate went backwards, crashing down onto the street, sending up a cloud of dust. Again, Luke turned to walk away, but Nate crawled on to all fours and grabbed Luke round the legs. The two men went down, rolling over.

A small crowd of townsfolk had come out of buildings and gathered at a safe distance to watch, Will Bullard, Chet Smith and Cyrus Yapp amongst them. Will glanced at Cyrus to see if the sheriff was going to do anything, but Cyrus looked reluctant to try to stop the contest.

For the next few seconds, fists flew. Then both men staggered to their feet, swinging punches, Nate getting the worst of it. Finally, exhausted, he fell back against the boardwalk, his eyes full of fury. His right hand moved towards his holster, but a hand grabbed his wrist.

'He ain't carryin', brother,' Mitch warned him, softly. 'It'd be plain murder, an' we got folks watchin'.'

'Soon fix that!' Nate snarled, and he pulled Mitch's gun from its holster and threw it at Luke's feet. 'Pick it up, mister!'

Luke stared down at the .45 without moving.

'*Pick it up*!' Nate screamed, his hand over his holster.

Luke sighed. Then, in one smooth movement, he dropped to the ground, scooped up the .45 and fired.

Nate's .45 was only half out of its holster when Luke's slug caught him between the eyes.

He died instantly, a look of astonishment printed on his face for eternity.

'Seems like there's been nothin' but trouble since you hit town, Frey,' Cyrus said. 'Three deaths in two days. Kind of a record around here. We're normally a peaceable town.'

They were sitting in the sheriff's office. Chet was standing in one corner, watching Luke with new respect, having never seen a man move so fast and shoot so accurately.

Nate Hurley's body had been removed from the street and the crowd had dispersed. Luke had dropped Mitch's .45 in the street and turned away. It had seemed for a moment as if Mitch might go for his gun and finish what his brother had started, but Cyrus had moved fast and gathered it up before the young man could do anything. He had left Mitch in the Scarlet Slipper, mourning the loss of his brother over a bottle of gut-rot whiskey and being comforted by Wanda.

'You saw what happened, Sheriff. No need for me to explain,' Luke said now.

'Oh, sure, it was self-defence, I'll give you that,' Cyrus allowed. His eyes narrowed. 'More'n you can say for Hettie and Pascoe.'

'I know nothin' about their deaths,' Luke said.

Cyrus considered him for several moments, rubbing a hand over his bristly chin. 'Just outa curiosity, where were you headin' when Nate Hurley stopped you?' he said at last.

'The bank,' Luke replied.

'You got business there?'

Luke lips twitched into a half-smile. 'Nope. Wanted a word with Mr ... Drummond, if that's really his name.'

Cyrus frowned. 'What you gettin' at, "if that's really his name"? What else would it be?'

'That's what I was gonna ask him,' Luke said. 'Seems like I know him from some place else, but if I do, he wasn't callin' himself Drummond there.'

'Oh, an' what was he callin' himself?' Cyrus asked.

'Simms,' Luke said. 'George Simms. 'Course I could be mistaken. That's what I was goin' to take up with him afore Nate Hurley stopped me in my tracks.'

'Was there some problem with this man Simms?' Chet interjected. 'Only Mr Drummond's a respectable member of the town, him bein' mayor and everythin'.'

'Now I think I'll keep that to myself for the time bein',' Luke said. 'I wouldn't want to stir up a hornets' nest if there ain't no need.'

Cyrus was about to say something when the door to his office swung open and Will Bullard walked in. The newspaperman's face was flushed and it was clear he was bursting to impart some news. Seeing Luke stopped him short, but only for a second.

'Just collected a wire from that editor friend of mine in Stanfield,' he told Cyrus. 'Got some more information on that train raid at Cutler's Pass.' He smiled. 'Mighty interesting it is, too.'

CHAPTER ELEVEN

Cyrus looked at Luke. 'You cottoned on to what Will here's talkin' about?'

Luke nodded. 'Word's got around town that there was a newspaper cuttin' in the dead real estate man's office, referrin' to a train robbery.'

'That's right,' Will said. 'And I've been in touch with the editor of that newspaper, the *Stanfield Gazette*. Well, it seems that although both the guard and the brakeman were shot in the raid, the brakeman didn't die straight away. He managed to say a few words to the conductor before he passed on.'

'What about?' Chet asked.

'About the raiders,' Will said. 'Seems two of them said a few words – and one of them had *a Bostonian accent.*'

Chet's jaw dropped. 'And Clyde Pascoe was a

Bostonian!' he said. 'He never made no secret of it. Even had a paintin' of the city on the wall in his office.'

'Right,' Will said. 'Only thing is, one of the others called the Bostonian "Adams".'

'Don't mean nothin',' Cyrus said. 'Could've changed his name when he came here.'

'I agree,' Will said. 'And I haven't finished, there's more. Apparently, there was a gambling man who spent a lot of time in Stanfield up until a few weeks before the train robbery who went by the name of Adams . . . *Clyde* Adams.'

Chet whistled. 'Gotta be the same man,' he said.

'No question,' Will agreed.

Cyrus looked across at Luke. 'What d'you reckon, mister? You don't look too surprised.'

Luke shrugged. 'Seems like Pascoe an' Adams were the same man, I agree.'

'There's another thing,' Will said.

'What's that?' Cyrus asked.

'Stanfield's a mining town, and it was a gold shipment that was taken from the train, right?'

'Right,' Cyrus said.

'And it was coming from that mine,' Will said. 'The *Gazette* editor confirmed that. So it's likely the information about the journey time and destination of the shipment was discovered by someone in

Stanfield, maybe by this Adams character.'

'So it's likely the other raiders came from Stanfield as well,' Cyrus said. 'Might even be worth tryin' to find out if any other people left Stanfield around the time of the raid, 'sides Adams. Could point to them bein' involved too.'

'It's possible,' Will said. 'What d'you think, Mr Frey?'

Luke shrugged again. 'Yeah, it's possible.'

'Tell me somethin', Frey,' Cyrus said. 'Where were you around midnight the night before last?'

Luke looked at him steadily. 'In bed, Sheriff. An' afore you ask, no there's nobody who could vouch for that.'

'An' last night, around the time Hettie was killed?'

'Seein' as I don't know what time that was, I can't tell you.'

'Likely it was after ten-thirty,' Chet informed him.

'Then the answer's the same,' Luke said. 'I was in bed. I ain't one for stoppin' up after ten o'clock unless there's good reason. Have to be up early to help Carrie prepare the breakfasts in the café. Now, if there's nothin' else, I'd like to mosey on to where I was headin' earlier.'

Cyrus stared at him, as if making up his mind. At last he said, 'Sure, I guess you can go. Just try an' stay out of trouble from now on, mister.'

They watched him leave and head across the street towards the bank.

'Interesting man, our Mr Frey,' Will said, after a few moments.

'How'd you mean, Will?' Cyrus said. 'You think he knows more about it than he's sayin'? You think he was involved?'

Will took his cherrywood pipe from his pocket and stuck it in the corner of his mouth. He chewed on it for a few seconds. 'Not directly, no. I don't think he was one of the raiders. But I'm thinking he's got some sort of interest in the matter.'

'Reckon he killed Pascoe?' Chet asked.

'Maybe,' Will said.

'What about Hettie?' Cyrus said. 'Reckon he killed her?'

'Can't see why he would,' Will said. 'Unless he *did* kill Pascoe and Hettie knew something and had to be silenced.' He frowned. 'It's the cutting that's interesting. The way I see it, the person who gave it to Pascoe wanted to get him worried. Maybe to the point where he would do something stupid; like give away the identities of the other raiders – *who could also be here in Jeopardy.*'

There was a silence as the other two men digested this.

'Jeez!' Chet said at last.

'So what you sayin', Will?' Cyrus said. 'That it was Frey who slipped the newspaper cuttin' to Pascoe? Hopin' that he'd do what you said – panic an' do somethin' that'd identify the other raiders?'

'Maybe,' Will said.

'But what's Frey's interest in the train robbery an' the raiders?'

Will smiled. 'Now that's the *really* interesting question,' he said. 'But I haven't got an answer.'

'So who killed Pascoe?' Chet wanted to know. 'We any nearer answerin' *that* question?'

'Could've been Frey,' Cyrus said. 'Or could've been somebody after the money Pascoe kept in his office.' He smiled.

' 'Ceptin' they didn't find it . . . 'cause I did.'

'*You* did?' Chet said.

Cyrus smiled smugly. 'Yep! Had me an idea where Pascoe might've hid his money for safe keepin', so I went back to his office an hour ago to see if I was right. An' I was.' He pulled open a drawer of his desk and took out a thick wad of notes. 'Near on a thousand dollars. Quite a stash, eh?'

'Hell's teeth! Where was it, Cyrus?' Chet said.

'The paintin'!' Cyrus said. 'It was spread out in the back of the paintin' behind a false panel.'

'The paintin' of Boston?' Chet said. 'The one on the wall?'

'The very same,' Cyrus said, nodding.

Will laughed. 'Good thinking, Cyrus!'

'Mm, but the question is, what do I do with the money? Pascoe didn't have no kin, as far as I know.'

'Oh, I reckon we can find a good home for it,' Will said, winking. 'Folks want a proper schoolhouse, and the church needs repairs to its roof. Yes, we'll find ways of spending it, don't you worry.' He took his timepiece from his waistcoat pocket and looked at it.

'Anyway, I should get back to the newspaper office. See you later, Cyrus. 'Bye, Chet.'

After he'd gone, Cyrus said, 'Reckon I'll go an' take a look round Hettie's room at the Scarlet Slipper. See if it tells me anythin' about Hettie's, er, customers last night. Seems most likely it was one of 'em who killed her.'

CHAPTER TWELVE

Luke came out of the bank and headed back towards Carrie's café. He hadn't been able to speak with George Drummond – whose real name he was now convinced was George Simms – because the banker had been out. Never mind, it would keep.

He wondered just how much the sheriff and the newspaperman had worked out about his interest in the Cutler's Pass train raid. Whether they'd guessed that he was the one who had passed the newspaper cutting to Clyde Pascoe-Adams. Luke didn't much care. The ruse hadn't worked anyway. Pascoe had died before he could let slip anything about the robbery that would have confirmed Luke's suspicions as to the identities of the other robbers.

But one thing Luke was almost certain about. Those very people were here in town.

Carrie looked relieved to see him when he got to the café. She had watched him go off with the sheriff and had been worried, she said.

'It's all sorted out,' he told her. 'Sheriff Yapp knows Nate Hurley was pullin' a gun on me when I shot him.'

'That don't settle things with Mitch Hurley,' Carrie warned him. 'You'll have to watch your back from now on, Luke.'

'Guess I will,' Luke said.

George Drummond had seen Luke leave the sheriff's office and head towards the bank. George had been coming down the street after leaving Gus Tute's barber shop where he'd had his morning shave. He had immediately changed direction and gone into the Scarlet Slipper, not wishing to come face to face with Luke, whom he was now certain knew more about him than was healthy.

It was in the saloon that he found Wanda consoling Mitch Hurley after the earlier shooting. Mitch's head was in his hands and Wanda had an arm around him and was speaking softly into his ear.

Gus had told George about the shooting whilst he'd been in the barber's chair. Secretly, George considered the hot-headed Nate Hurley's death no particular loss to the town, but he kept his thoughts to himself. Especially in the saloon as he'd always got the impression that Wanda had a soft spot for the twins.

He went across to the bar and ordered a drink. After some minutes, Cyrus Yapp came in. He glanced around the room and, seeing Wanda with Mitch, headed towards the bar.

'Morning, Sheriff,' George said. He nodded towards Mitch. 'Terrible business about Mitch's brother.' He shook his head slowly. 'Seems to me, there's been nothing but trouble since that man Frey arrived in town.'

Cyrus nodded. 'Yeah, there has.' He ordered a beer and, when he'd taken several sips, said, 'Frey reckons he knows you from some place.'

George blinked rapidly, then raised his eyebrows. 'Oh, really? From where?'

'He didn't say,' Cyrus answered. 'Reckoned you went by a different name then, though.'

'What was that?' George asked. He was avoiding Cyrus's eye.

'Simms,' Cyrus told him.

George almost dropped his glass, but managed to keep his voice steady. 'Then he's clearly mistaken. Drummond's my name, always has been.'

Cyrus nodded again. 'Yeah, seems he's mixin' you up with some other *hombre*.' He swallowed a mouthful of beer, then went on. 'Seems Clyde Pascoe was involved in that train robbery all right. Will Bullard's been in touch with the editor of the *Stanfield Gazette*.' And he repeated much of the conversation he'd had with the newspaperman.

George listened intently. 'And you think Frey might have killed Pascoe,' he said when Cyrus had finished. 'Well, I'll be damned.'

'He ain't got an alibi for the time of the killin'. Reckons he was in bed, but can't prove it. Same thing with Hettie. Can't *prove* he didn't kill her, either. Though, truth be told, I can't see a connection between the two murders.'

George's head was awhirl with thoughts. 'Doesn't mean there isn't one,' he said.

'True,' Cyrus said. 'I'll be watchin' our Mr Frey kinda closely from now on.'

Across the room, Mitch had got up from the table and was leaving through the batwings. Wanda was watching him, an anguished look on her face. After a moment, she walked across to the bar.

'Guess Mitch is real cut up about his brother,' Cyrus said.

Wanda sighed heavily. 'Yeah,' she said. 'I've been tryin' to console him, but it ain't easy.'

'If you can't do it, nobody can,' Cyrus said. 'Always treated those boys like sons, you have, Wanda. Guess you've been able to see good in 'em where other's can't.'

Wanda seemed startled by the suggestion and waved it away. 'No, no, just bein' neighbourly.'

George couldn't imagine why anybody would want to be neighbourly to a pair of rattlesnakes like the Hurley twins, but he didn't say so.

'Mind if I have a look round Hettie's room, Wanda?' Cyrus asked. 'Don't reckon it'll shed much light on who killed her, but I guess I should check it out.'

'Go ahead,' Wanda told him.

She and George watched the sheriff mount the stairs before Wanda said, 'Did *you* see Hettie last night, George?'

George felt his face get hot. 'What? No, no, not last night.'

Wanda's eyes narrowed, then she smiled. 'Know somethin', George? You're a terrible liar.'

George began to bluster. 'What? I-I don't know what you mean! I-I spent the evening with Harmony, and—'

Wanda put a hand over his lips. 'I ain't the sheriff, George. So, come on, you can tell me. Remember, I know a few things about you that folks around here would be surprised to learn, don't I?'

'Now Wanda, you promised—!'

'Yeah, yeah, I know.' She put a placating hand on his arm. 'It was pillow talk an' I never repeat pillow talk' – her voice hardened – 'lessen I have to.'

George's own hand shook as he gulped down the rest of his drink. 'All right, yes, I did see Hettie last night,' he admitted, 'but she was already dead!'

Wanda stared at him. 'Go on,' she said.

'Well, I planned on going up the back stairs, as usual, but there she was, lying in the alleyway.' George took his handkerchief from his pocket and wiped the sweat from his forehead. 'I swear to God, Wanda, she was dead.'

Did she believe him? He couldn't be sure. That was the trouble with Wanda, her face never gave away her feelings. She said nothing, just continued to stare at him.

'Listen, I have to get to the bank,' he said at last. 'I'll see you later.'

She watched him leave, a half-smile on her face. After a moment, Eddie came along the bar to join her.

'Pour me a whiskey, Eddie,' Wanda said. 'I've got some serious thinkin' to do.'

'Mr Drummond looked kinda worried,' the barkeep said.

Wanda nodded. 'George has a few skeletons in his

cupboard an' he's worried some of 'em are about to escape,' she said.

CHAPTER THIRTEEN

Mitch lived in a one-room adobe shack on the edge of town. It was a squalid little building with a leaking roof and crumbling walls. There were a few sticks of furniture and an oil lamp. Until today, he'd shared the place with his brother, now he had it to himself.

He sat slumped in a chair with a jug of rot-gut liquor from which, every few moments, he took a gulp.

Ever since his twin's showdown with Luke Frey, Mitch had replayed the incident over and over in his mind trying to make sense of what had happened.

'The bastard!' he muttered. 'He didn't have to kill Nate!'

In some ways, he blamed himself for Nate's death. After all, he'd encouraged his brother to 'hassle' Frey, hadn't he? And he should have known that, with Nate's fiery temper, things would quickly spiral into violence. But what he couldn't have anticipated was the speed with which Frey had moved when he'd scooped up Mitch's .45 and let loose. Where in hell had the critter learned to move and shoot like that?

However, Mitch knew what he had to do now. For word was getting around town that Luke Frey seemed to know things about the Cutler's Pass train raid, maybe even knew the identity of the raiders. And that could prove dangerous to Mitch and others, so Frey had to be stopped.

Mitch and his brother had got through their share of the robbery in a matter of months. Clyde Pascoe had won a chunk of it in games of poker, much to Mitch's chagrin. He should have remembered that Pascoe had been a professional gambler for most of his life. Still, now the critter was dead.

Had that been Frey? Had he discovered that Pascoe was one of the gang members and killed him? Which raised the question: what was Frey's interest in the train robbery? Was he seeking some sort of revenge? If so, why? He wasn't one of the owners of the gold mine, so the money hadn't been his to lose.

Then, from somewhere in Mitch's drink-soaked, befuddled memory there emerged a recollection of a violated woman, stretched out on the floor of a cabin, clothes torn and pleading for mercy. A young mother whose cries had haunted Mitch's dreams for months after the event. Not so his brother, who had been the violator and, finally, the woman's killer. Nate had shrugged off the incident without a qualm.

Was the woman the connection with Frey? Could she have been his wife or sister?

Suddenly, Mitch began to feel like a condemned man awaiting execution.

All afternoon, George Drummond had brooded in his office. He'd eaten no lunch, and had snapped at his clerk whenever the old man had tried to approach him with papers for signing or a decision to be taken on a loan.

The more George had thought about what Cyrus Yapp had told him that morning, the more he'd come to realize Luke Frey represented a threat to his whole existence here in Jeopardy. That fact in itself had been sufficient to create a pain in his gut that seemed to cut him in half.

There were no two ways about it. *Something had to be done about the man.*

Now, sitting in his study at home, he remembered the lace handkerchief he'd taken from his wife's bedside drawer and a plan began to form in George's mind. And the more he thought about it, the more it appealed to him.

After coming to a decision, he opened a drawer of his study desk ... and removed the bloodstained handkerchief from it. The letter 'H' was hand-stitched into one corner of the cotton fabric.

'I'm going to let the law take care of you, Mr Frey,' George muttered to himself. 'I'm going to watch you hang!'

CHAPTER FOURTEEN

Faith Eastwood was owner and proprietor of Jeopardy's one and only hotel, The Gemstone. When she and her husband had bought it from the previous owner it had been more of a flophouse-cum-brothel, and without a name. But Faith had almost single-handedly transformed it into a respectable, modestly comfortable establishment that served good food and guaranteed clean sheets on the beds for all its guests.

After Jeremy died of a heart attack, Faith had, for a brief moment or two, been half-tempted to sell up and move on. But Carrie Mitford (of all people, considering they were to some extent business competitors) had persuaded her to remain in

Jeopardy. It was a decision Faith had not regretted.

The two women had formed a strong friendship after Jeremy's death and, to her amusement, Faith realized that Carrie now seemed to be attempting a spot of matchmaking, involving her new lodger and helper.

It was late evening and they were sitting at a table in Faith's private living-room in the hotel, drinking tea, munching shortbread and playing chequers, Carrie having closed her café for the night.

'He ain't afraid of a bit of hard work, I'll say that for him,' Carrie was saying.

Faith moved a chequer but made no comment.

'Strong, too,' Carrie went on. 'The sort of man who'd make a woman feel safe and secure, an' keep her warm on winter nights.'

Faith hid a smile. 'Sounds just the man for you, Carrie. Maybe you should—'

'Nah!' Carrie said laughing. 'I've been a widder-woman for too long now. Too set in my ways. 'Sides, he's nearer your age than mine. What are you, Faith, twenty-six, twenty-seven?'

'Twenty-eight,' Faith admitted.

'There you are then!' Carrie said. 'Time's marchin' on, an' Luke's in his early thirties. Just right!'

Faith laughed. 'Oh, Carrie, you're incorrigible!'

'I am, am I? Whatever that means. Well, I'm tellin,' you. You could do a whole lot worse than Luke Frey.'

They concentrated on their game for some minutes before Faith said, 'Mr Frey's got a sad, faraway look about him, I've noticed. As though he's suffered some tragedy, some terrible misfortune in the past.'

Carrie nodded. 'Know what you mean, I've noticed it myself. But whenever I ask him where he was or what he was doin' afore he came to Jeopardy, he clams up. "Tell you sometime, Carrie," he says. "Not now." And that's as far as I get.' She glanced sideways at her friend. 'Maybe you'll do better later.'

'Later?' Faith frowned. 'How'd you mean?'

Carrie licked her lips and cleared her throat. 'Now don't go gettin' uppity, or anythin', but I took the liberty of invitin' Luke over later.'

'Over *here?*'

' 'Sright. Told him about this tasty shortbread you baked this mornin'. Said you'd be only too happy to let him sample it.' She glanced at the longcase clock in the corner of the room. 'Eight o'clock. Reckon he'll be here any minute now.'

'Carrie Mitford, you're – you're—'

'Incorri— whatever-it-was? Yeah, well, I guess I am. But seems to me *somebody*'s gotta get things movin' on the marriage front, lessen you want to be a widder-woman like me for the rest of your life.'

'Marriage!' Faith almost choked on her piece of shortbread. 'When did I ever tell you I was looking for another husband?'

'Well, you should be, fine young woman like you,' Carrie told her. 'An' furthermore—'

It was as far as she got before there was a knock at the door.

CHAPTER FIFTEEN

Carrie gave a triumphant smile, in contrast to Faith's red face and look of discomfort.

'That you, Luke?' Carrie called out. 'Come on in! You're in luck, we ain't eaten all the shortbread.'

The door opened slowly, hesitantly, before the long-legged, angular figure of Luke Frey appeared.

'Evenin', Mrs Eastwood. Carrie.' He hovered uncertainly in the doorway holding his Stetson.

'Good evening, Mr Frey,' Faith said, suddenly – *embarrassingly* – aware that her pulse rate had increased. 'D-do come in and have a seat.'

Carrie pulled a chair away from the table, placing Luke between herself and Faith. A manoeuvre which Faith did not fail to notice judging by the look she gave her friend.

'Finished tidyin' up at the café,' Luke informed

Carrie. 'Finally got shot of Carl Darby.'

'Carl likes to linger after his supper,' Carrie said. 'He's a bachelor-man. Nobody to go home to.' She eyed Faith. 'Kinda sad, that, don't y'reckon, Faith? Bein' on your lonesome all the time?'

'It's something you get used to,' Faith replied carefully. 'Don't you agree, Mr Frey.'

'Please, call me Luke,' he said.

'Then you must call me Faith,' she said. 'But don't you agree, Luke, that sometimes solitude has its advantages. Gives you time to think, to reflect.'

'Maybe,' he said. His expression had turned sombre and he avoided her eye. 'Although it depends where your thoughts . . . turn.'

'Oh, well yes, of course,' Faith said, colouring. 'I didn't mean . . . that is. . . .'

She rose from the table to fetch a cup and saucer, and to pour him a cup of tea. An awkward silence lay over the room for some moments before Carrie cleared her throat and spoke.

'Luke, don't you think it's about time you came clean with folks about your – well – *sadness*,' she said bluntly. 'It's plain there's *somethin'*, an' we're your friends, Faith an' me. An' anythin' you wanna tell us ain't gonna go no further than this room, if'n that was the way you wanted it.'

He looked from one to the other of them. 'It

would be,' he said quietly. 'For the time bein',
anyway.'

'Then it *will* be,' Carrie said. 'So come on, my
good friend, unburden y'self.'

Luke gave a sigh of acquiescence. 'OK,' he said.
He paused for a moment, the went on, 'I had me a
wife, once. A daughter, too. But not any more. My
daughter died, and my wife was murdered. *Raped* and
murdered.'

Faith gave a sharp, horrified intake of breath.

'How did it happen?' Carrie prompted gently,
when he seemed reluctant to go on.

'My wife, Martha, and my daughter, Rose, were on
their way to see Martha's mother upstate, in
Cannersville,' Luke said. 'It's a small town north of
here, and it had just got itself a rail link. Martha
thought it'd be a good time to go an' see her folks
and let them see their granddaughter for the first
time. I didn't mind, although there was too much
work on hand for me to go with them.' He stared
down at his hands, a bleak look on his face. 'Dear
God, the times I've cursed myself for not goin' with
them! Anyway . . . we had a small homestead at the
time, nothin' fancy, but a decent little place. We'd
worked hard, made it nice. Martha had a . . . a
garden which she loved tendin', and—' He broke
off, suddenly overcome.

Carrie put a hand on his arm. 'Go on if you can, Luke.'

He nodded. 'Anyways, they were takin' the train to Cannersville when it was derailed by a bunch of raiders. Place called Cutler's Pass. The loco and passenger coaches were thrown down an embankment. Plenty of folk were killed straight away, includin' Rose. But Martha, she . . . well, she wasn't. But, accordin' to the train conductor, one of the raiders took her as the bunch of them rode off with the $80,000 gold shipment. Just scooped Martha up like a sack of corn, he said, and rode off. A posse found her body a week later, in a dilapidated old cabin in the hills. Reckoned it was where the gang had holed up for a day or so after the raid. Like I said, they'd . . . abused her, before they killed her.'

He glanced at the two women before going on. Faith's face was the colour of chalk, her eyes wide with horror, and her hands were shaking. Carrie's face was a mask of controlled fury.

'Filthy pigs!' she said.

'Yeah,' Luke said, 'an' I've spent the last five years tryin' to track 'em down. Sold my homestead an' linked up with the detective who was investigatin' the robbery on behalf of the minin' company.'

'Five years?' Faith said. 'You've been hunting these – these men for five years?'

'Yep,' Luke said.

'And you've landed up in Jeopardy,' Carrie said. 'Why here?'

'Because I reckoned the raiders ended up here,' Luke said.

He sipped his coffee.

Faith stared at him, alarm spreading across her face. 'What makes you think that?' she asked after a moment.

Luke put a hand on her arm. 'Didn't mean to scare you none,' he said. 'But me an' the detective spoke to some of the survivors of the crash. Got no place. No leads, nothin'. Except for one person, who reckoned there were *five* members of the gang not four, as most other witnesses seemed to think. This woman reckoned she saw a fifth person up on a knoll, away from the railway line, watchin'. Anyways, one of the survivors seemed to be less forthcomin' than the others. A big man, ex-jailbird fresh out of Yuma prison. Well, I reckoned it was because a detective was askin' the questions that he was bein' tight-lipped, so I went back and saw him on my own.

'Seems he landed up just yards from the caboose, when he was thrown through the window of the coach he was sittin' in. Heard a couple of the raiders talkin' as they mounted their horses before the getaway. Heard one say somethin' like ". . . won't get

90

us in jeopardy". Now *he* thought same as me, that the raider was sayin' that what they'd done wouldn't get them in *danger. . . .*'

' 'Cause that's what the word means!' Carrie said, catching on fast.

' 'Xactly,' Luke agreed.

'But what made you think the man was referring to a town?' Faith asked.

'Sheer chance,' Luke said. 'It was months later when I met a guy who'd passed through a town called Jeopardy. It set me thinkin'. Could it have been a *place*, the raider was talkin' about? An' if it was, just imagine what four – or maybe five – people comin' to a town with a stash of money could do. Damnit, they could nigh on *own* the town, if they wanted to.

'An' then I started askin' questions in Stanfield – that's the town near where the minin' company was operatin', an' I reckoned whoever planned the raid had probably been livin' there.'

'Makes some sorta sense, I guess,' Carrie said.

'Yeah, well I discovered there'd been a gambler by the name of Clyde Adams – livin' an' operatin' in Stanfield but originally from Boston.'

Carrie's eyes lit up. 'Boston? So you're talkin' about Clyde Pascoe?'

Luke nodded. 'I learned today that one of the raiders had a Boston accent. So, yeah, it had to be the same critter.'

'Did you discover anything else about the people living in Stanfield?' Faith asked.

'Not much,' Luke admitted. 'Adams – or Pascoe as we knew him – left the town about a week before the train raid and never returned.'

'But ended up here in Jeopardy!' Carrie said.

'Seems that way,' Luke said. 'Only other thing I discovered was that two more *hombres* left about the same time as Adams. Twin brothers by the name of Nate and Mitch Harvey. An' they were a coupla hell-raisers by all accounts.'

Carrie gasped. 'The Hurley twins!'

Luke nodded again. 'An' it's my bet it was one or both of 'em who . . .abused an' murdered Martha.' His eyes hardened. 'Which is why I ain't sorry I killed Nate Hurley this mornin'.'

Faith was shocked to the core and was having difficulty holding in her emotions. Carrie, a tougher breed, looked full of suppressed rage.

'Anyways,' Luke went on, 'I was hopin' to learn who the other raiders were from Clyde Pascoe.'

'You – you asked him?' Faith said.

'Nope, he would have denied knowin' anythin' about the train robbery even if I'd got him to admit he was Clyde Adams; an' I had no proof he was one of the raiders. So I tried to rattle him by slippin' a newspaper cuttin' about the robbery under his door the evenin' he was killed. I kinda hoped he'd be unnerved enough to go runnin' to one or more of the other raiders – maybe includin' the head of the gang – an' in doin' so tell me who they were. But somebody shot him afore he had a chance.'

'Too bad,' Carrie said. She was thoughtful for several moments before she went on. 'You say there were five raiders all told?'

'Apparently,' Luke said. 'Like I said, one of 'em – the leader almost certainly – never took part, just watched from the knoll.'

'It could have been somebody passing by,' Faith said. 'Somebody who didn't want to get involved.'

'What kind of person wouldn't help out after the robbers had gone?' Carrie said. 'No, I reckon Luke's right. Whoever was watchin' was one of the gang.'

'I guess so,' Faith said, quietly.

'So two of 'em – Pascoe an' Nate Hurley – are dead, an' Mitch Hurley was another,' Carrie said. 'That leaves two more.'

'Yeah,' Luke said.

'And – and you believe these men may be living here in Jeopardy?' Faith said, her voice shaking.

'I can't be certain,' Luke admitted. 'It's just a feelin' I've got.' He sighed. 'There, now you know the whole thing.'

'Are you sorry you told us, Luke?' Carrie asked, hesitantly.

'No,' Luke said after a moment. 'No, I guess not.'

CHAPTER SIXTEEN

Mitch eased himself into a more comfortable position on the rooftop of the feed store, then picked up the Winchester and nestled it against his shoulder. His head was clearer now, the effects of the liquor having worn off after a short sleep and a pot of strong coffee.

From this vantage point he could see the alleyway at the back entrance to Carrie's Café as well as the upstairs windows at the rear of the building, one of which he guessed was Luke Frey's room. Both windows were in darkness.

It was almost ten-thirty and he'd been stretched out behind the feed store fascia board for best part of an hour. Clouds hid all but a handful of stars in the night sky and the temperature had dropped to near freezing. The street below was empty, apart from a stray dog and the occasional tumbleweed blowing through.

Earlier, when he'd been nursing a cup of coffee in the Scarlet Slipper and staring out into the street, he'd seen Luke Frey cross and enter the hotel. At first Mitch had been surprised, but then he'd remembered Carrie Mitford was a friend of Faith's and was probably attempting a spot of matchmaking, Faith being a widow-woman and Frey a man who apparently had no wife or family. It was something Carrie was known for – matchmaking. Hadn't she been instrumental in finding the local parson a wife a few months back? Only person she didn't try to get hitched was herself.

For reasons Mitch wouldn't have wanted to reveal to anyone, he didn't want Luke Frey getting too friendly with Faith Eastwood. He kinda liked Faith and, in wilder moments, imagined sharing her bed. Which had given him another cause to put an end to Frey's life.

Suddenly he was aware of movement in the alley-way. A figure was approaching the back door of the café – and judging by the shape, it wasn't Luke Frey.

'George Drummond!' Mitch muttered. 'What'n hell is he doin'?'

He watched as Drummond glanced around before opening the café's back door and slipping inside.

Nobody locked doors in Jeopardy so it was no surprise to Mitch that Drummond had been able to gain access so easily. What was puzzling was *why* the banker found it necessary to sneak in late at night when the building was empty.

Mitch was even more intrigued a few minutes later when he saw the light from a lamp appear in one of the upstairs rooms.

'I'd bet my last dollar that's Frey's room!' he thought. 'But what's Drummond up to?'

Almost immediately, the lamp went out and the room was in darkness again. Moments later, George reappeared in the alleyway and hurried away into the night.

'Damn me!' Mitch muttered.

He tried to think. What possible reason could the fat banker have for entering Frey's room when Frey wasn't there? To look for something? Something Frey had that Drummond wanted? Something *incriminating*? Wanda always reckoned George Drummond had some skeleton in the cupboard. In fact, Mitch was damn sure Wanda knew what it was, although she'd never said. But did Frey know Drummond's secret?

Mitch chuckled to himself. 'If so, George, I may be about to do you a favour,' he thought.

Luke and Carrie left the hotel just after eleven

o'clock and began walking back to the café. Carrie was wrapped in a thick shawl against the cold but was bareheaded.

'Nice lady, Faith,' she said. 'Too nice to be a widder-woman. Make somebody a good wife one of these days.'

Luke smiled to himself but said nothing. He knew what Carrie was up to. But the fact was, something about the hotel owner puzzled him. For a start, she had seemed unsettled by the way the conversation had been going, especially when Luke had spoken of his wife's death and what had led up to it. OK, most women would be shocked by what had happened to Martha, it was true, but Faith Eastwood had seemed *alarmed* by his story. As if she was afraid of it happening to her? No, dammit, that didn't make sense.

'Got somethin' on your mind, Luke?' Carrie said, interrupting his thoughts.

'What? No, not really,' he said.

They were a few steps from the back entrance to the café. Carrie stopped and turned towards him.

'You regrettin' tellin' us all that about your wife an' kid?' she said. ''Cause if'n you are, you don't have to worry about me or Faith repeatin' it.'

Luke shook his head. 'Nope,' he said. 'Although, yeah, I'd just as soon you kept it to yourselves, for the moment anyway.'

Her shawl had slipped off the back of one shoulder and Luke leaned forward to replace it.

It was a movement that saved his life.

The downward trajectory of the shot missed his head by a fraction but embedded itself in Carrie's back, the sound of the explosion echoing in the darkened street a split second later.

CHAPTER SEVENTEEN

Carrie's eyes widened and her mouth opened in a silent scream as she began to fall. Luke caught her, pulled her into the doorway behind them, and pushed the door open all in one movement.

Another shot followed, splintering the edge of the door frame, as Luke gently laid Carrie on the floor. After the shooting with Nate Hurley, he had taken to wearing his gun again – something he'd not felt the need to do since he'd arrived in Jeopardy until that day. Now he pulled it from its holster and flattened himself against the doorframe as he tried to see where the sniper was located. After almost a full minute, he saw a figure dart across the roof of the feed store and was able to pin-point his would-be assassin's position.

Luke was debating whether to set off towards it or to tend to Carrie when he heard feet running down the boardwalk in the street. Moments later, Pete Buss and Doc McReedy appeared in the alleyway.

'I heard shootin',' Pete said. He had his nightshirt stuffed into his pants and was bare-footed.

Doc McReedy had pulled a robe over his night-shirt and was clutching his black bag. 'Me too,' he said. 'Figured I might be needed.'

'You are,' Luke said, urgently. 'Tend to Carrie while I try to run down the critter who fired on us.'

Mitch tossed the Winchester to the ground and scrambled down the side of the feed store after it, cursing his luck. He was certain his shot had been just inches away from its intended target, but it had ended up cutting down Carrie Mitford.

Hell!

Gathering up the rifle, he started to run along behind the buildings on that side of Main Street. He was confident Frey hadn't been able to identify him as the shooter, although he was also sure the other man would quickly guess who had tried to kill him.

'But guessin' ain't provin',' Mitch told himself.

If he could just get to his shack before Frey reached it. . . .

Luke had no doubt he'd been the shooter's target, not Carrie. And he had a pretty good idea who the failed marksman was – which was why he was heading towards Mitch Hurley's shack.

He was twenty yards from it when he saw the half-stumbling figure of Mitch reaching for the door.

'Hurley!' he cried.

Mitch reacted instinctively, turning and firing the Winchester from the hip. The shot sang wild and high, missing Luke by a couple of feet. Even so, Luke dropped to the ground as Mitch thrust open the shack door and rolled inside.

Luke lifted his .45 and fired, but his shot whined harmlessly over Mitch's head before the other man kicked the door shut. In the centre of the street, Luke felt too exposed now that Mitch was safely inside. Running in a crouch, he zig-zagged across to the side of the shack and flattened himself against the front wall.

He could hear Mitch cursing, and the sound of some piece of furniture being shoved hard against the shack door. Luke held his position, breathing steadily.

Far away, down the darkened street, he could see shadowy figures appearing from one or two of the buildings, but nobody seemed anxious to get any nearer the shack. He wondered whether the sheriff or Will Bullard was amongst them. If they were, they were keeping their distance like the others.

The shack's single window was already cracked across one corner. Reversing the Colt in his hand, Luke reached out and used the butt to smash the rest of the glass. He immediately dropped to a crouch under the window and flattened himself against the wall again. At the same moment, another shot – from a six-shooter this time – rang out over his head.

'You ain't goin' no place, Mitch!' Luke yelled. ' 'Cause there's no place to go – 'ceptin' maybe to hell!'

'You murdered my brother, Frey!' Mitch screamed. 'Now I aim to make you pay for it!'

'An' you an' your brother murdered my wife, Mitch!' Luke shouted. 'Tell me, did you both rape her first, or was it just Nate?'

Silence.

Then, 'What-what'n hell you talkin' about, Frey?'

'The train raid, Mitch, remember? Cutler's Pass? Five years ago? One of you picked up my wife an' rode off with her after you took the gold shipment. Not somethin' you're likely to forget, Mitch. Me neither.'

The soft sound of curses came from inside, followed by more silence.

'Remember, Mitch?' Luke said.

'Sure, I remember,' Mitch said at last. 'Figured you were here for that reason. Only it weren't me, it was Nate who. . . .' his voice trailed off.

'Don't make no never-mind, Mitch,' Luke said. 'You were there. You could've stopped him.'

More silence.

Then the barrel of a .45 suddenly came into view in the corner of the window frame, angled downwards. It coughed smoke and lead.

The angle was sharp, but not sharp enough. The bullet hit the dirt six inches from Luke's feet. He quickly rose to his full height and fired through the broken window. There was a yell as the bullet found its target, but a reply came immediately as the other .45 let loose a stream of three shots. The last caught Luke's shoulder, spinning him round so that he hit the dirt hard.

He rolled and fired back as Mitch's head and shoulders appeared in the dark square of the window. The bullet took Mitch in the throat and he slumped forward over the shards of broken glass.

Luke breathed heavily in the silence of the night. Then, out of the shadows behind him, figures began to appear. At the forefront of the little crowd was Cyrus Yapp.

'Frey!' he yelled. 'We need to talk!'

Luke sighed.

CHAPTER EIGHTEEN

Doc McCreedy was still wearing his nightshirt but had stuffed it into a pair of creased and frayed pin-stripe trousers.

'She's bad, but she'll make it,' he said, in answer to Luke's question about Carrie's state of health. 'I got the bullet out, but she lost a lot of blood in the process. Needs rest. Won't be cookin' no meals for a spell.'

He was dressing the flesh wound to Luke's shoulder in the downstairs room of his house that served as his surgery. Carrie lay sleeping on a cot in the next room.

The other two occupants of the 'surgery' were Will Bulllard and Cyrus Yapp. The sheriff was perched on the edge of a scrubbed pine chair, turning his Stetson over in his hands. He waited until Doc

McReedy finished tending Luke's wound, then stood up.

'I need an explanation from you, Frey,' he said. 'I heard snatches of what you were sayin' to Mitch afore you killed him, but not all of it. Somethin' about your wife an' the train robbery at Cutler's Pass?'

Luke pulled on his shirt and nodded his thanks to McReedy. The doc looked from one man to the other, then said, 'Guess I'll go check on my other patient whilst you two chew the fat.'

After he'd gone Luke repeated the story he'd told Carrie and Faith earlier that evening.

'So you're here in Jeopardy to avenge your wife's murder?' Will said when Luke had finished.

'Yeah, but I was kinda hopin' to find enough evidence for the law to take care of things,' Luke said. 'I ain't no vigilante, although I came prepared.'

'You sure as hell know how to use a gun,' Cyrus said. 'How come?'

'Practice,' Luke replied. 'Five years of practice. I figured I might be up against some men who were useful with a gun, so I got myself primed for trouble.'

Cyrus sighed. 'So far you've seen off three of the raiders – Pascoe and the Hurley twins.'

'I had nothin' to do with Clyde Pascoe's death,' Luke said. ''Ceptin' I slipped the newspaper cuttin' under his door, for the reasons I've explained. But

I'm guessin' the cuttin' had nothin' to do with his murder.'

'Why d'you say that?' Will enquired.

'Happened too quickly,' Luke said.

'There was still time for him to have talked to somebody about it,' Will said. 'Maybe the *leader* of the gang – the fifth man you mentioned. Pascoe could've got panicky, realizing he'd been identified as one of the raiders, and the gang's leader could've decided to silence him before he did something stupid. Something that would point the finger at *him – the fifth man.*'

'Maybe,' Luke said. He didn't sound convinced.

'Are you sayin' you reckon the remainin' two raiders are livin' here, in Jeopardy?' Cyrus wanted to know.

'Can't be certain of that,' Luke said. 'But at least three of them – the Hurley twins and Pascoe – came from Stanfield. Could be the plan was for all five of 'em to set up afresh someplace, maybe with a view to workin' together on another robbery when funds got low. They must've felt pretty happy about the way things turned out at Cutler's Pass. Enough to make 'em confident they could do it again.'

'We've always suspected that the Hurley boys pulled the odd stage hold-up, but that's all,' Will said, glancing at Cyrus.

The sheriff looked uncomfortable. 'We've never been able to prove anythin', Will, you know that,' he said.

'Pretty damn sure, just the same,' Will said. He looked at Luke. 'Have you got any thoughts about the identity of the two remaining raiders?'

'Maybe one of 'em,' Luke said. 'But I wouldn't want to point the finger without bein' sure, so don't go pressin' me.'

Will yawned. 'OK. Anyway, it's time I got back to my bed. You're certainly helping me with things to write about in this week's edition of the *Clarion*, Frey.'

'Yeah, but I'd be glad if'n you could be a little *less* helpful,' Cyrus told Luke. 'Four killin's in two days is too damn many!'

CHAPTER NINETEEN

Luke stayed at the doc's house overnight, mostly dozing at Carrie's bedside. Doc McReedy took to his own bed soon after the newspaper editor and the sheriff left.

Carrie stirred and woke slowly as the first shimmers of morning sunlight striped the room's floorboards. She turned her head to see a weary-looking Luke watching her.

He smiled. 'First off, Doc McReedy says you're gonna be fine,' he said.

'Wh-what happened?' she said.

'You caught a bullet meant for me,' Luke said. 'Tell you more later when you're feelin' more yourself. Anythin' you want?'

'Water,' Carrie said. 'Mouth's drier than a desert.'

'I'll go get you some,' he said.

He went through to the kitchen where he was surprised to see Faith Eastwood with the doctor. She was wearing a shirtwaister dress and strands of her chestnut-coloured hair protruded from under a neat little straw bonnet.

'I came to see how Carrie was?' she explained to Luke. 'I heard the shooting last night but didn't connect it with you or Carrie. I thought it was the Circle Y boys having their fun again. It was only this morning I learned what happened when my desk clerk told me.'

'She's awake,' Luke said. 'Wants some water. Maybe you'd like to take it through to her. I figured I'd go an' open up the café. Can't cook like Carrie, but I can rustle up a few eggs an' ham, an' some pots of coffee, should any folk come wantin'. First though, I've got a wire to send to an out-of-town sheriff. Had me an idea.'

'A wire?' she looked at him questioningly.

For a moment, he seemed about to elucidate, but then changed his mind. 'Tell Carrie I'll be back soon,' he said.

'I'll do that,' Faith said. She smiled at him. 'I-I may drop by the café a little later, to-to tell you how she is and . . . and have a few words.'

He looked back at her, feeling his cheeks colouring. 'OK,' he said, after a moment. 'I'll be there.'

111

It was still dark when Stump Stimpson secreted his pot-bellied body behind the water trough outside the livery and waited. He stretched out his club-footed leg and eased himself into a position where he could peer around the edge of the trough. He saw a buck-board swinging along the street, and two cowboys heading back to the Circle Y after sleeping off a drunk in the saloon, but moments later the street was empty.

It was daylight by the time he saw Faith Eastwood enter Doc McReedy's house and then, some minutes later, saw Luke Frey appear in the doorway. Stimpson glanced around to be certain there were no onlookers, then brought the big Colt into line as Luke Frey crossed the street.

Maybe if he'd taken the advice of the person who was paying him and who had been sitting across the table from him in the saloon the night before; maybe if he hadn't had that extra slug of gut-rot whiskey to steady his nerves before coming out into the street, his aim would have been straighter and he might not have lingered with his head above the parapet. As it was, he missed his target by a good ten inches and forgot to duck after he'd fired. Giving Luke time to turn, draw his own .45 and fire at Stimpson's protruding head. Unlike Stimpson, Luke didn't miss.

He walked quickly over to the water trough and, using his booted foot, turned over the slumped form of his would-be assassin. To Luke, the man was a stranger.

Carl Darby appeared from the side door of the livery.

'Jeez, Mr Frey,' he said. 'Somebody sure as hell wants you dead!'

Luke nodded towards the motionless form. 'You know him?'

'Sure,' Carl said. 'Name's Stump Stimpson. No-good layabout.'

'And sometime paid killer?' Luke queried. He had stooped down and taken a fifty-dollar gold piece from Stimpson's vest pocket. 'Seems my life comes relatively cheap to somebody.'

'Jeez!' Carl said again.

Luke sniffed. 'Guess I'd better go an' inform Sheriff Yapp. He ain't gonna like it – another dead body.'

He was right. Cyrus heard his story and groaned.

'You stay in town much longer, Frey, an' there ain't gonna be many townsfolk left!' he growled. 'OK, get out of here! Chet, go see Abel an' get him to get Stump outa the street afore the rest of the town wake up.'

Luke and the young deputy left the sheriff's office together.

Chet grinned. 'Cyrus is developin' an ulcer, havin' you around, Mr Frey!' he said.

Luke smiled back. 'Seems so.'

George Drummond heard about the deaths of Mitch Hurley and Stump Stimpson from the chief teller at the bank. Like Faith Eastwood, he'd heard the shooting the previous night and had assumed it was probably a drunken Circle Y boy shooting up the town, as they were wont to do. He'd slept through the early morning shooting initiated by Stump Stimpson.

As soon as he learned the truth, George made a beeline for the sheriff's office, delighted that a situation he was trying to engineer was playing right into his hands.

Cyrus poured himself a third cup of coffee and raised a questioning eyebrow towards Chet. The young deputy shook his head. He pushed his empty cup aside.

'So this Frey fellah's been trackin' down the Cutler's Pass train robbers for five years?' Chet said. He was sitting in the chair on the opposite side of Cyrus's desk. Cyrus was half-slumped in his swivel

114

chair looking like a man badly in need of a good night's sleep.

'Yup,' Cyrus said, sipping his coffee and grimacing at the bitter taste. 'An' seems like we've been keepin' company with at least three of 'em, here in Jeopardy.'

'An' the other two might be here as well,' Chet said.

Cyrus shrugged. 'Who knows? Frey says he can't be certain. Don't seem likely to me, but then—'

He broke off as the office door opened and Jeopardy's mayor strode in like a man on a mission.

'Things are getting out of hand around here, wouldn't you say, Cyrus?' he said. 'It's about time you did something to stop it!'

CHAPTER TWENTY

'Hello, George,' Cyrus said calmly. 'You look as though you've got a hornet in your pants. Somethin' up?'

George Drummond removed his planter's hat and settled himself in the chair Chet had swiftly vacated on seeing the banker enter. The deputy moved over to the window and leaned against the sill.

'Just heard about last night's killing,' George said. 'This man Frey's brought nothing but trouble to the town.'

'Wasn't Luke Frey who started things last night, Mr Drummond,' Chet said. 'Mitch Hurley took a pot shot at him. Missed, but hit Carrie Mitford.'

'And *why* was Mitch shooting at Frey?' George asked, staring straight at Cyrus and not even deigning to give Chet a sideways glance.

'Prob'ly 'cause Luke Frey shot Nate,' Cyrus allowed, 'but it was Nate who drew on Frey first.'

'Mitch was also a good, er, friend of Hettie, and he told me plainly that Nate knew Frey killed her. Said Nate was going to get proof.' George delivered this lie smoothly and without batting an eyelid. He gazed steadily at the sheriff.

Cyrus stared back, his coffee cup poised halfway to his mouth. 'Proof? What kinda proof?'

George shook his head slowly. 'Mitch didn't say. Only that Nate planned to look for it in Frey's room over the café. Guess he never got around to it before he died. But he was certain something was there.'

'Why would Luke Frey kill Hettie?' Chet put in.

George continued to ignore the deputy, addressing Cyrus direct. 'Maybe Hettie knew something about Clyde Pascoe's murder. Something that pointed a finger at Frey being the killer, so he had to get rid of her.'

Cyrus exchanged a look with Chet. *Say nothing about Luke Frey's connection with the Cutler's Pass train robbery* was the unspoken message. *Or about the Hurley twins and Pascoe being involved.* Chet gave the smallest of nods.

'So what're you suggestin', George?' Cyrus asked.

'I'm suggesting you do what Nate failed to do,' George said. 'Search Frey's room for evidence that

117

he murdered Hettie.'

'Well now, I don't know—' Cyrus began.

'I'm not *asking* you,' George cut in. 'I'm *advising* it. I grant you some folk around here didn't think too highly of Hettie and her, uh, line of work, but they'll want to see justice done. They'll want to be sure you're doing your job.'

With that, he stood up and put his hat on. 'I'm sure we can all rely on you to do the right thing, Cyrus,' he said, as a parting shot.

Chet did not speak for some moments after George Drummond left, but eventually he said, 'You goin' to do what our esteemed mister mayor *advised*, Cyrus?'

' "*Esteemed*",' Cyrus repeated with a half-smile. 'Now that's a two-dollar word to describe a two-bit banker, Chet.' He sniffed. 'Even so, I guess I'd better take a look around Frey's room. But I aim to do it alone, an' when he ain't there. No sense rilin' the fellah.'

' 'Specially when the fellah's as fast on the draw as he is,' Chet added. 'Eh, sheriff?'

Faith Eastwood was about to open the door of Carrie's Eating House when she saw the hastily scribbled notice stuck on the glass – '*Shut until Carrie's back on her feet*'. She debated whether to return to the

118

hotel or go to the rear entrance of the café and see if she could make herself heard by calling up the stairs.

However, she was saved the trouble of making a decision when Luke himself appeared at the mouth of the alleyway alongside the café.

'Howdy, Faith,' he said. 'Lookin' for me?'

'I came to see how you were managing at the café,' she said.

'I decided that fixin' meals for the folk of Jeopardy is beyond my capabilities,' he said. 'Reckon they'll have to go hungry until Carrie's back.'

'How is she?' Carrie asked.

'I'm on my way to Doc's now to check on her,' Luke said. 'You want to come with me?'

'I have to get back to the hotel, but I can walk part way with you,' she said. 'I'll go to see Carrie this evening.'

'Probably best,' Luke said. 'Don't want to tire her out with too many visitors.'

The street was deserted, the heat from the midday sun having driven most folk indoors. They walked in silence for some minutes, then Luke said, 'It must've been tough after you lost your husband, runnin' the hotel alone.'

Faith nodded. 'Yes, well, you have to carry on, don't you?' she said. 'And that's when Carrie became a real good friend to me.'

119

'Had you an' your husband been in Jeopardy long?' Luke said.

'Less than a year,' she said.

'How did he die?' Luke asked.

She hesitated, then said, 'Heart attack. Collapsed in the street.' She seemed anxious to change the subject. 'Tell me, do you really believe Clyde Pascoe and the Har – Hurley twins were part of the gang who raided the train at Cutler's Pass?'

He looked at her steadily. 'Yeah,' he said slowly 'I'm sure. Why?'

She shook her head. 'No reason,' she said quickly. 'It-it's just a little frightening to think the town has been harbouring men like that.' They had arrived at the entrance to the hotel, but she seemed in no hurry to go in.

'Could be harbourin' two more, if my guess is right,' Luke said. 'Just need to figure out who they are.'

'Do you have any ideas?' she asked.

'Not right now,' he said, after a moment.

'Well, I'll leave you to go and check on Carrie,' she said, turning away. 'Tell her I'll come and see her later.'

Luke watched her go into the hotel, a thoughtful expression on his face, before going on towards Doc's house.

'Reckon she knows somethin' she's not tellin' me,' he muttered to himself. 'Now why would that be?'

Cyrus and Chet watched through the sheriff's office window as Luke walked away from The Gemstone hotel and made his way towards Doc McReedy's place.

'Seems kinda friendly with Mrs Eastwood, don't he?' Chet observed.

'Can't blame him for that,' Cyrus said. 'Faith's a fine woman.'

'True,' Chet agreed.

'Anyway, might be a good time to go an' search his room,' Cyrus said.

'Want me to come an' keep watch in case he comes back unexpected?' Chet asked.

'Yeah, good idea,' Cyrus said.

The two men left the office and walked swiftly down the street. Chet waited at the end of the alleyway as Cyrus entered through the back door of the café. The sheriff climbed the stairs to the rear of the building and quickly identified which room was Luke's.

It contained a bed, a low chest of drawers with a washbowl on top, a rail for hanging clothes and a small wooden table and chair.

Cyrus felt uncomfortable ferreting through Frey's

things, but it took him less than three minutes to discover what he reckoned George Drummond had been talking about.

He found it tucked at the back of a drawer – a blood-stained lace handkerchief with the letter 'H' stitched in one corner.

'*Hettie*'s!' he said to himself. 'Oh, hell!'

CHAPTER
TWENTY-ONE

Carrie had just eased herself into a sitting position in bed when Doc McReedy came to tell her she had a visitor. Her heavy-lidded eyes reflected the pain she was still suffering, but she nodded her assent. She was wearing a paper-thin white nightdress with frayed edges over her bandaged chest. The nightdress had once belonged to the Doc's mother, which, he had told Carrie, he kept for emergencies like hers. On hearing this, Carrie had made a mental note to make and present the doc with a couple of new night-dresses when she was able.

'You up to visitors?' he asked her. ''Cause I can tell him to get lost if you ain't.'

'No, it's OK,' she said, her voice little more than

a croak.

She gave Luke a weak smile when he came in and perched on the side of the bed.

'No sense askin' if you're OK, 'cause I can see you ain't,' he said. He grinned. 'But at least you're breathin'.'

'They tell me . . . it was you . . . Mitch was aimin' at?' she said, breathing heavily between words.

'Damn right it was,' Luke said. 'An' I'm real sorry you caught it, but the critter ain't gonna be shootin' anyone else ever again.'

He gave a brief account of the events at the Hurleys' shack. Carrie listened with a grave look on her face.

'Told you that Mitch . . . wouldn't be forgivin' you killin' Nate,' she said when he'd finished.

'An' you were right,' he allowed.

'The café?' she asked.

'Shut for the time bein'. I had me a try at makin' a few breakfasts, but Pete Buss, Carl Darby an' a couple of others weren't too impressed. Guess they're used to your cookin'.'

She grimaced, adjusting her position, and he helped her rearrange her pillows before going on. 'Tell me, how long ago was it that Jeremy Eastwood died?' he asked.

Carrie frowned. 'Now why're you wantin' to know

that?' she said.

'Just interested.'

She studied him for several moments, then said, 'Must be . . . nigh on four years ago, maybe five.' She smiled. 'You thinkin' . . . of makin' a play for Faith, Luke? Could be . . . good timin'.'

'Nope, I ain't ready for anythin' like that,' he told her.

'Pity,' she said. 'Faith needs . . . a good man.'

'Mm, well, she'll be comin' in to see you this evenin',' he said.

Her eyes closed momentarily. 'Guess I . . . could use some sleep. . . .'

'Sure,' Luke said, removing himself from the edge of the bed. 'You take it easy, Carrie.'

He went out through the kitchen where Doc McReedy was making a pot of coffee. He nodded towards a seat at the kitchen table when he saw Luke.

'Coffee?' he said.

'Be nice,' Luke said, and sat down. 'Carrie gonna be OK? She looks kinda weak.'

'What d'you expect? She took a slug in her back. She's damn lucky to be alive.' He looked accusingly at Luke. 'A slug meant for you, I'm thinking.'

'Yeah, I know,' Luke said. 'An' I feel bad about it.'

Doc was silent for a moment, then he said, 'Why're you here, Luke? What brought you to Jeopardy?'

Luke sighed. 'It's a long story,' he said. 'Not sure you'd want to hear it.'

'Try me,' Doc said. 'I ain't goin' no place for now.'

CHAPTER
TWENTY-TWO

Cyrus emerged from the back of the café, a deep frown creasing his forehead.

'Find anythin'?' Chet asked him.

'Yeah,' Cyrus said. 'An' I kinda wish I hadn't.' He held up the blood-stained lace handkerchief for Chet to see. The deputy whistled.

'Hettie's?' Chet said.

'Looks like it,' Cyrus said.

'Guess we'd better find Mr Frey an' ask him,' Chet said.

'Guess so,' Cyrus said. 'He still with Doc McReedy?'

'Ain't seen him come out,' Chet said.

'I'll go back to the office,' Cyrus said. 'You go an'

tell Frey I want to see him when he's finished his visit with Carrie. Say nothin' about the handkerchief.'

'OK,' Chet said.

The two men parted and Cyrus made his way across the street. Once inside his office, he took a glass and a bottle of red-eye from a desk drawer and poured himself a drink. He eased himself into his chair and waited, thoughts circling in his head. Up until a few days ago, his job had been without complications. Now he had three murders on his hands and a whole heap of unanswered questions.

Some ten minutes later, the office door opened and Chet came in with Luke Frey. The latter looked mildly puzzled but otherwise unconcerned.

'What can I do for you, Sheriff?' he asked.

Cyrus pushed the blood-stained handkerchief across the desk. Luke looked at him for a moment, then picked it up. He turned it over in his hands and examined the initial in the corner.

'This what I think it is?' he said.

'Seems clear enough,' Cyrus said. ' "H" for Hettie, I reckon.'

Luke nodded. 'Possible. So where did you find it?'

'Well, now, that's the thing, y'see,' Cyrus said. He paused, then went on, 'I found it in your room over Carrie's café.'

Luke stared at him. 'You've been in my room?

How come?'

'Seems Mitch Hurley knew there'd be some incriminatin' evidence tucked away some place in your room, pointin' to you as the killer, but he died afore he could go an' find it.'

'Mitch tell you that?' Luke asked.

'Not Mitch, no.'

'Who then?' Luke said.

Cyrus smiled and shook his head.

'Never mind, I can guess,' Luke said. 'It was George Drummond, right?'

Cyrus shrugged and said nothing. Luke looked at Chet, but the deputy was staring at his feet.

'Let me get this straight,' Luke said. 'Drummond comes in here with some tale about Mitch knowin' there'd be some sorta proof that I killed Hettie if you went lookin' in my room. So you high-tail it over to Carrie's an' poke around in my things. An' lo an' behold you find a blood-stained handkerchief with the letter H stitched on it. So, right off, you decide it must be Hettie's an' I must have killed her. That about right?'

Cyrus shrugged again. 'Kinda adds up, don't you reckon?'

Luke sat himself down in the chair opposite Cyrus. 'Just ask yourself a few questions, Sheriff,' he said. 'One: assumin' I did kill Hettie – which I didn't, by the way – why would I keep such an incriminatin' piece of evidence in my room for somebody to find? Why wouldn't I have just left it with Hettie's body? Two: George Drummond tells you that Mitch planned to get "proof" from my room that I killed Hettie. But how *could* Mitch have known the handkerchief would be there? Three: why does it have to be Hettie's handkerchief an' Hettie's blood? Gotta be more than one lady in this town whose name starts with the letter H. Remind me, sheriff, what's Geroge Drummond's wife's first name?'

Cyrus and Chet looked at one another.

'Harmony,' Chet said, after a moment.

'What you suggestin'?' Cyrus said. 'That our mister mayor *planted his wife's* handkerchief in your room to make you look like Hettie's killer? Why would he do that?'

'Because George Drummond – whose real name is George *Simms* – knows I've recognized him for who and what he really is. An embezzler who had to get out of the bank where he was workin' an' the town where he was livin' in one helluva hurry.'

Cyrus and Chet were suddenly all ears. 'Where was that?' Cyrus asked.

'Doyle County, coupla hundred miles west of here,' Luke told him.

Cyrus nodded. 'I've heard of it.' He frowned at

Luke. 'You sure about this?'

'Damn right, I am,' Luke said. 'Wire the sheriff there, an' ask him. His name's Bassett.'

'I surely intend to do that,' Cyrus said. 'Meantime, you're to say nothin' about this to nobody. An' don't leave town.'

Luke chewed his lip, thought for a moment, then said. 'I'll do better than that, I'll take up residence in one of your cells.'

'Eh?' Cyrus looked confused.

'Listen, put the word out that you've arrested me for Hettie's murder. Then get Will Bullard to come an' see me. Tell him I've got a story for his paper. Oh, an' if a wire comes for me, maybe you could collect it.'

'You expectin' one?' Cyrus asked.

'Yeah,' Luke said.

'Where from?'

'Stanfield,' Luke answered.

'Wanna tell me about it?' Cyrus asked.

'Nope,' Luke said. 'Not yet, anyway.'

Cyrus stared at him. 'You sure you know what you're doin'?'

'I'm sure,' Luke said.

CHAPTER TWENTY-THREE

George Drummond observed events through the window of his office in the bank. He saw the sheriff and his deputy cross the street to Carrie's café, saw Cyrus vanish down the alleyway whilst Chet kept watch and, some time later, saw Cyrus showing Chet what he'd discovered in Luke Frey's room. He watched the two men go their separate ways then, a short time afterwards, watched Chet escort Frey from Doc McReedy's across to the sheriff's office.

All appeared to be going according to plan, George thought as he sat at his desk. Even so, for reasons he couldn't immediately pin down, a smidgen of unease lurked in his mind. It identified itself a few minutes later in the form of an important question. *Did Luke Frey know who he was, and thus know about the embezzlement?* The answer, it began to seem to George, was almost certainly, *Yes.*

Suddenly, his plan of setting up Luke Frey in order to be rid of him seemed liable to backfire. For one thing, would Frey tell Cyrus Yapp what he knew had happened in Doyle County? Would he use the information to divert attention from the blood-stained handkerchief and Hettie's death? Answer: *almost certainly.* Would Yapp believe Frey? *Maybe, but he'd probably check out the story by wiring the sheriff in Doyle before doing anything.*

George began to sweat. He felt as if a noose was gradually tightening around his neck.

Could he bluff his way out of this, or was it time to move on? Go east, maybe. If he was right, and Yapp checked with the sheriff in Doyle before taking any action, it meant that he had about twenty-four hours in which to get together as much cash as possible, and high-tail it to the railway depot at Yellow Fork. From there he could begin his getaway east.

One thing was certain, he told himself. He wouldn't be taking Harmony with him. The nagging old cow could take her chances.

He was suddenly aware of movement in the street outside and saw Cyrus come out of the sheriff's office and head off in the direction of the Chinese café at the other end of the street. It was lunchtime and, with Carrie Mitford's eating house closed for business, the little Chinaman was the next best bet. What was satisfying to George was that Cyrus had not headed for the bank to confront him with whatever Frey had told him, and that Frey himself had not come out with the sheriff. Which could only mean one thing, couldn't it?. That Frey was safely tucked away in Jeopardy's jail, charged with Hettie's murder.

George looked at the clock on his office wall. Harmony would be out lunching with a couple of the townswomen she played whist with some afternoons. So this might be a good time to go home and pack a few things ready for a hasty departure the next day.

He turned away from the window and, for the next few minutes, concentrated on signing the letters and papers his clerk had brought in earlier.

Busy with his paperwork, George did not see Cyrus Yapp make a detour to the *Clarion* office. After a short time, the sheriff came out again and walked down the street to the telegraph office. He was there some minutes before exiting and heading off towards the Chinese eating house again.

Will Bullard emerged from the *Clarion* office soon after. He made a beeline towards the town jail.

*

134

Luke was taking a nap on a cot in one of the cells, his hat tipped over his forehead. The hot midday sun streamed through the barred window above his head.

It was only when Will put a hand on his shoulder that he roused.

'Cyrus reckons you've got a story for me,' Will said. 'That so?' He looked quizzically at Luke.

The cell door was open behind him and Chet was leaning against the doorpost, equally curious.

Luke sat up and gathered his thoughts. 'I told you about my wife an' kid an' the train robbery,' he said to Will.

Will nodded. 'I plan to feature your story on the front page. It'll be all over town by this time tomorrow.'

'Good,' Luke said. 'I want you to add somethin'.'

'OK,' Will said.

'I want you to say that I'm pretty sure I know the name of the gang leader, but that I ain't sayin' it, at least not at the moment. Make out like you an' the sheriff are tryin' to persuade me to reveal it an' that you reckon I won't be able to hold out for more'n a day or two longer.'

'*Do* you know the identity of the gang leader?' Will asked. 'Or is this just a ruse to flush him out? You're expecting him to try and get to you before you say

135

anything, I presume.'

Luke nodded. 'That's the plan. An', no, I ain't *sure* who the leader is, but I've got a fair idea.'

'I'm about to join Cyrus for lunch,' Will said. 'I'll tell him.' He turned towards Chet. 'Meantime, you'd best keep a close eye on your, uh, prisoner.'

'Sure,' Chet agreed. 'Reckon by the time the *Clarion*'s on the streets, he'll be a sittin' duck.'

CHAPTER TWENTY-FOUR

It soon got around that Luke Frey was being held in the town jail for Hettie's murder. When word reached Doc McReedy, he decided not to tell Carrie. He didn't want her shocked or upset. Unfortunately, he was out tending a sick child when Faith Eastwood called to see Carrie that evening, and she unwittingly let slip the news.

Carrie was incensed. 'That's plum crazy!' she said, painfully hoisting herself up in the bed. 'Luke's no killer, not unless he's forced to draw against rattlesnakes like Nate Hurley! Cyrus is loco!'

'They're saying Luke might have got angry when Hettie wouldn't—' Faith Eastwood's face coloured. 'That is, when he asked her to. . . .' Her voice trailed off with embarrassment.

'Hogwash!' Carrie said. 'If'n Luke . . . uh . . . availed himself of her . . . uh . . . services – an' I don't believe he ever did – then he wouldn't have asked Hettie to do anythin' *disagreeable.*'

Faith sighed. 'I'm sure you're right. But it seems the sheriff found something of Hettie's in Luke Frey's room. Chet Smith admitted as much to Pete Buss, and Pete told me when I was at the mercantile late this afternoon.'

'What did the sheriff find?' Carrie demanded.

'A handkerchief,' Faith replied. 'With blood on it.'

'How do they know it was Hettie's?'

'It had the initial "H" embroidered in one corner,' said Faith.

Carrie gave a snort of disgust. 'Since when did saloon girls own fancy handkerchiefs with their initials embroidered on 'em? It could belong to anybody.'

'But what was it doing in Luke Frey's room?' asked Faith.

'Somebody put it there, to make Luke look guilty,' Carrie said firmly. 'Maybe one of the Hurley twins afore they died. It's more'n possible one of *them* killed Hettie for the reasons you were suggestin' earlier. Then Nate or Mitch could've *planted* the handkerchief in Luke's room.'

'I suppose that's possible,' said Faith. She hesitated, and Carrie noticed.

'You got somethin' on your mind, Faith?' she asked.

'It's just that – well – Luke's been hunting down the men who killed his wife and daughter,' Faith began.

'The train robbers, you mean,' Carrie said. 'What about it? You suggestin' it was one of them who killed Hettie and who's' tryin' to get Luke hung for her murder?'

'I don't know,' Faith said. 'We don't know how much Luke has discovered. He was certain the Hurley twins and Clyde Pascoe were members of the gang. Perhaps he's close to discovering the identity of the other two.'

Carrie frowned. 'Maybe you've got somethin' there. An' maybe Hettie knew somethin' about the robbery, too. Killin' her an' gettin' Luke hung for her murder would be a good way of silencin' both of 'em.' She looked at Faith's worried face and put a hand on her arm. 'It's nice to see you frettin' about Luke. He's a good man, Faith. Maybe when all this is over an' Luke's proved innocent, you an' he. . . .' She let the sentence drift.

Faith shook her head. 'I don't think so, Carrie.' She stood up quickly. 'I must be getting back to the hotel. I'll call in again tomorrow.'

'Yeah, thanks, Faith,' Carrie said. 'Maybe there'll be better news about Luke by then.'

'You've got a visitor,' Cyrus said.

Luke looked up and saw Faith Eastwood standing in the cell doorway. He stood up.

'Thank you, Sheriff,' she said. It was a dismissal, and Cyrus recognized it as such and went back onto his office.

'You don't *look* as though you're under arrest,' she said to Luke, nodding at the open cell door.

He smiled. 'That's because I'm not. Well, not officially. Guess you could say the sheriff's got me here for safe keepin'.'

'Safe from who?' she said.

'Not sure right now. Reckon I'll know by this time tomorrow evenin'.'

They were silent for several moments, Luke watching her carefully.

'I came to see if you wanted anything,' Faith said at last. 'Food or clothes or anything.'

Luke looked unconvinced. 'Really?'

Her face flushed. 'Well, I also thought I'd report on Carrie's condition.'

Luke waved a hand towards the cot. 'Maybe you'd like to sit down.'

She perched on one end and Luke leaned against the bars of the cell, waiting.

'Carrie's going to be fine,' she said. 'She just needs to rest. She's real mad at the sheriff. She doesn't believe for a moment that you murdered Hettie, regardless of the handkerchief Cyrus Yapp found in your room.'

'It was planted,' Luke told her. 'I'm just not certain who planted it, although I've got a pretty good idea.'

'You have?' she said.

Luke nodded. 'Best if I keep my suspicions to myself for the time bein', though.'

'Do – do you need anything?' Faith asked.

'Nope,' Luke said. 'I'm OK.' He looked questioningly at her. 'How about you? Got somethin' on your mind?'

She opened her mouth to speak, then closed it again. 'No, nothing,' she said, after a moment.

Silence. Then Luke said, 'Thought maybe you wanted to tell me about your husband.'

'Jeremy?' she said, her face colouring again. 'Why would I want to talk about him?' She stood up quickly. 'I-I have to go. I-I've things to do . . . back at the hotel. I'll tell Carrie not to worry about you; that you're fine. 'Bye, Luke.'

He watched her leave, a thoughtful expression on

his face. After some minutes, Cyrus appeared in the cell doorway.

'Got yourself a female admirer, I reckon.' he said, grinning. 'Can't say as I remember Mrs Eastwood ever comin' to see one of my jailbirds afore.'

'I think she came for a reason, then changed her mind,' Luke said. 'She seems kinda worried about somethin'.'

CHAPTER TWENTY-FIVE

By late morning the next day, copies of the *Clarion* were all over town. Two people took a particular interest in Will Bullard's story about Luke, and what the latter knew – but for the moment wasn't telling – about the Cutler's Pass train robbery, and about the identity of the gang members, including their leader. Both had reasons to feel nervous, but only one decided to take decisive action.

Chet walked away from the sheriff's office and headed down Main Street. Cyrus watched him from the window of his office. When Chet turned down a side alley, he called back to the cell, 'OK, I'm goin' out now! Just watch yourself!'

'OK!' Luke yelled back.

Cyrus made his way across the street to the Scarlet Slipper. Eddie the barkeep looked up, surprised.

'A might early for you, ain't it, Sheriff?' he said. 'Or are you wantin' to speak to Wanda? She's out back.'

'Nope,' Cyrus said. 'Just needin' a drink.'

Eddie nodded sympathetically. 'Reckon you do, at that. All these killin's. Still, you've got the critter responsible for murderin' Hettie, an' that's somethin'.'

'Yep,' Cyrus agreed.

'That right he knows somethin' about the Cutler's Pass train robbery, an' that's what brought him to Jeopardy?'

Cyrus nodded. 'Seems so. He ain't talkin' at the minute, but he will afore I've finished with him.' He looked round and nodded towards a table by the window. 'Bring the bottle an' a pack o' cards across, Eddie. Reckon I'll have me a quiet game of solitaire, afore I go back.'

A third reader of the *Clarion* who had reasons to fear Luke Frey's loose tongue was about to make a hasty exit from Jeopardy. George Drummond had his bags packed, a money belt stuffed full of banknotes under his shirt, and a horse and buggy ready to take him to

144

the nearest rail depot at Yellow Fork.

Harmony was still in bed, complaining of one of her many headaches, and George was happy to let her stay there. By the time she eventually rose – usually around noon – he would be gone.

The rear of George's house led on to an alley, and it was here his horse and buggy awaited him. Now, struggling towards it with a bag in each hand and a third under one arm, he was suddenly aware of someone moving out of the shadows of the nearby buildings.

'Goin' someplace, Mr Drummond?' Chet asked, casually.

A startled George dropped the bag from under his arm and swung round. 'What'n hell—!' he began.

Chet smiled and stepped forward to pick up the bag. 'Kinda jumpy, ain't you, Mr Drummond?' he said.

'Never mind that,' George snapped. 'What're you doing snooping around the back of my house?'

'Well now, Sheriff Yapp had a feelin' you might be takin' a trip some place, kinda secretive like. Fact is, he wants to have a word with you afore you leave.'

George shook his head. 'I can't help that. I-I've important business in Yellow Fork. Tell him I'll come and see him when I get back.'

Chet pasted a crooked smile on his face. 'Can't do

that, Mr Drummond. Cyrus said as you might wanna leave without seein' him, an' he told me to *insist*.' He put a hand on the butt of his holstered .45, as if to emphasize the point.

'This is ridiculous!' George blustered. He threw his bags into the back of the buggy and made a move to climb up into it – and suddenly found himself looking down the barrel of Chet's .45.

George's shoulders slumped in surrender. He knew exactly why Cyrus Yapp wanted to see him. There would be a wire from a sheriff in Doyle County, confirming that George Drummond was in fact George Simms, and that he had embezzled twelve thousand dollars from the Doyle County bank five years ago.

'Put that damn gun away!' he told Chet. 'I'll come with you, but I'll not have you march me up Main Street at the point of a damn gun!'

Chet grinned and holstered his weapon. 'Good decision, Mr Drummond,' he said.

CHAPTER
TWENTY-SIX

A figure carrying a Winchester eased open the rear door of the sheriff's office, breathing heavily, having half-run along the backs of the buildings on the south side of Main Street.

Carefully, the figure opened a rear door and stepped into the back room where Cyrus slept and kept his few belongings. From there it was simple to open the door through to the office a crack and confirm that there was no sign of the young deputy, then cross quickly to the door that led to cells behind.

The figure pushed the door open wide . . . and stared. All three cells were empty.

Suddenly, the butt of a .45 crashed down on the

Winchester, knocking the rifle to the floor.

Luke scooped it up and stepped out from behind the door. 'Howdy, Wanda,' he said. 'Come to finish off the job Stump Stimpson couldn't? The job you paid him to do after you heard that Mitch had failed to kill me?'

Wanda Decker gave a howl of rage. 'Bastard!' she screamed. She made to step forward but checked when Luke pointed the .45 at her ample bosom.

'Best not,' he said. 'I ain't as easy to kill as Hettie.'

She stared at him. 'So, what're you gonna do?' she asked after a moment. 'Kill me?'

'Only if you try to leave,' Luke said. 'Otherwise I plan to leave it to the sheriff to decide. Prob'ly get you hanged for Hettie's murder even if he can't prove you were the leader of the train robbers' gang. Which you were, right?'

Wanda was silent for several seconds, then said, 'Ain't gonna be easy to prove that, or that I killed Hettie.'

'You did though, didn't you?' Luke said.

Wanda shrugged, 'Stupid little cow tried to black-mail me,' she said. 'That damn fool Nate let slip I planned the raid on the train. She figured I'd still have enough of the money left to part with some. She wanted a thousand dollars.' Wanda laughed. 'Stupid bitch!'

'So you killed her.'

'Sure I did,' Wanda said.

'So that's like . . . a confession,' Luke said.

Wanda laughed again. 'Sure, but it's your word against mine.'

'Not quite,' said a voice from behind her.

Wanda wheeled round.

'I heard it, too, Wanda,' Cyrus Yapp said. 'Which means you'll hang.' He drew his own .45 and motioned towards the nearest cell. 'Inside,' he told her.

Wanda didn't move.

Cyrus sighed and thumbed back the safety on his gun. 'Gonna save me the trouble of a trial, Wanda?'

Wanda stared at him for several seconds, then walked towards the cell. To reach it, she had to pass by Luke, who had holstered his Colt.

In one movement, she hurled her substantial body sideways, knocking him to the floor and yanking his .45 from its holster. He tried to level the Winchester at her but she wriggled behind him and, using his body as a shield, she fired at Cyrus. The bullet clipped the sheriff's forearm before he managed to get back into his office, kicking the door together.

Luke struggled to pull away from Wanda's grip, but now she had the barrel of his .45 against the side of his head.

149

'Get up,' she told him. 'Carefully.' She moved away from him and stood up, the .45 levelled at his chest.

Luke slowly got to his feet. 'What're you gonna do, Wanda? Kill me? Go ahead. Mitch or Nate or both killed my wife an' kid. I ain't got a whole lot to live for.'

'An' you killed them,' Wanda said. 'That alone would be reason enough for me to kill you.'

'Why?' Luke said. 'What were they to you, other than a coupla crazy animals?'

She did not answer immediately. When she did speak, her voice had dropped to a dull monotone. 'Nate and Mitch were my brother's sons. He was a widower. His wife died of a fever. I brought up Mitch and Nate after he died in a minin' accident. An accident that should never have happened.'

'Minin' accident?' Luke repeated.

'Yeah,' Wanda said, bitterly. 'An' the owners of the mine didn't care nothin' about safety or about the men they sent underground. Hank, my brother, died with fifteen other miners when a tunnel roof collapsed. They were buried alive.'

'An' this was the same mine the gold shipment on the train came from,' Luke said, suddenly understanding.

'Yeah,' Wanda allowed.

150

'Which, for you, made takin' it some kinda twisted poetic justice.' Luke was watching her.

'Nothin' *twisted* about it,' Wanda said.

'So you brought Nate and Mitch up,' Luke said.

'Yeah, I did,' Wanda said, defiantly. 'Me, a madam in a cheap whorehouse!' She snorted. 'How about that? But I couldn't handle 'em. Too damn wild. But useful when it came to the train robbery, 'cause they knew how to handle a gun.'

'Not clever enough to plan it, though,' Luke said. 'Whereas you were.'

She nodded, then smiled. 'Especially when one of the managers of the mine let slip about the gold shipment when he was – how can I put it? takin' his pleasure of me.'

'But you had no intention of doing the actual *robbin'*,' Luke said. 'So you needed some extra help for Nate and Mitch. Which was where Clyde Pascoe, or Clyde Adams as he was known then, came in. How'd you manage it, Wanda? He owe you money?'

'Me an' half of Stanfield,' she said.

'Then there was the fourth man,' Luke said.

'Yeah, he—' Wanda stopped suddenly, becoming aware that he was stringing her along, hoping the sheriff would go and get help. 'Quit stallin'!' she said. 'You're my ticket out of here, an' there's things to do. Things to arrange. You hear that, Sheriff?' she yelled.

'I can hear it all, Wanda,' Cyrus said from the other side of the door. 'But there ain't no things to arrange. You ain't goin' no place.'

'Then I kill Frey!'

'Makes no difference to me,' Cyrus said. 'I ain't his keeper. Fact, he's been trouble ever since he arrived in town. It's been like the Grim Reaper paid Jeopardy a visit, with people dyin' all over the place.' He sniffed loudly.

'A catalyst for change, that's me,' Luke said, chuckling and seemingly unworried by Cyrus' indifference to his well-being.

'Tell me somethin' though, Wanda,' Cyrus said. 'You kill Pascoe?'

Wanda laughed. 'Nope, not me. My guess is that it was our friendly Mayor Drummond. Clyde was blackmailin' him, did you know that? Told Drummond he had "written proof" that Drummond was an embezzler. All lies, o'course. Clyde had nothing of the sort. But Drummond has a past he don't want people to know about.'

'So I heard,' Cyrus said.

'So he got jumpy. Did me a favour when he killed Pascoe, though,' Wanda said. 'Clyde was gettin' nervous himself, over some newspaper clippin' somebody had sent him.' Her eyes narrowed and she looked at Luke. 'That you?' she asked.

Luke nodded.

'Wondered if it was,' Wanda said. She became more businesslike. 'Now listen up, Sheriff. You're gonna—'

Suddenly the sound of breaking glass came from behind her and she whirled to see the barrel of a Winchester poke through the barred window of Luke's cell. The face behind the rifle was that of deputy Chet Smith.

As Wanda turned Luke's .45 towards him, Chet fired.

A hole appeared in Wanda's forehead and her gaze became a fixed stare before she dropped to the floor.

Luke turned and saluted Chet, then stood over the saloon owner. He shook his head slowly.

'Like the sheriff said, Wanda,' he muttered. 'You ain't goin' no place. 'Ceptin' maybe to hell.'

Cyrus came into the cell. He glanced down at Wanda then looked towards the window. 'Good timin', Chet,' he said. 'Been to see George Drummond? Got him with you?'

'Yeah,' Chet replied, grinning. 'He's sittin' out here in his buggy awaitin' his fate. We heard the shootin' comin' from the jail and Mr Drummond has obliged me by waitin' until I'd helped you out.'

Cyrus laughed, then turned to Luke. 'Got that wire you were expectin' he said.'

Luke nodded. 'Good.'

CHAPTER TWENTY-SEVEN

Faith Eastwood was in the lobby of The Gemstone when Luke came in. She and the clerk at the desk were studying an accounts book. She looked up and her expression was a mixture of relief and fear when she saw Luke's face.

'Can we talk?' he asked her.

She swallowed. 'Of course, Luke,' she said. She led the way across the lobby.

'Coffee?' Faith asked, when they were in her private living-room.

Luke shook his head. Two hours had passed since the events at the jail. 'No, thanks. You heard about Wanda?'

She stood with her hands clasped in front of her,

avoiding his eye. 'Yes.'

'And George Drummond?'

She nodded. 'Doc McReedy told me when I went to see Carrie. I-I was shocked.'

'But not shocked to find out about Wanda's past?' he said. 'Well, no, I don't reckon you were.'

'I-I don't—' she began.

'Come on, Faith,' he said gently. 'Tell the truth. You knew Wanda planned the train robbery at Cutler's Pass, didn't you? You knew because *your husband was the other raider.*'

She opened her mouth, seemingly about to deny it, then closed it again. 'Did Wanda tell you?' she said quietly.

'Nope,' Luke said. 'I guessed when you started gettin' anxious about what I was findin' out about the gang. I asked myself why that would be. Then I wired the sheriff in Stanfield an' asked if any other people had moved away from the town around the time Pascoe an' the Harvey twins left.' He held up a piece of paper. 'He replied. Told me about three others. The madam of the local whorehouse, Wanda Harvey. Also the woman who ran a boardin' house, an' her – an' this is the sheriif's words – "good-fer-nuthin' husband". Their names were Faith and Jeremy Spencer.

'Boardin' house to hotel ain't much of leap for my

imagination, Faith. I knew straightaway he was talkin' about you.'

Faith sighed. 'Sheriff Cavendish was right about Jeremy,' she admitted. 'He never amounted to anything. A drunk who spent most of his time at Wanda Harvey's whorehouse or gambling our profits away at one of the town's saloons with the Harvey twins.'

'Go on,' Luke said.

'It was Nate who persuaded his aunt to let Jeremy come in on the train robbery,' Faith said. 'I knew nothing about it until after it had happened. And, believe me Luke, I knew nothing about the – about your wife.'

'I believe you,' he said.

'Jeremy suddenly had more than $10,000 and an urgent need to get out of Stanfield fast,' Faith went on. 'He knew Sheriff Cavendish was no fool and would link the money to the train robbery. "We have to get out of Stanfield, Faith," he said. And, stupidly, I agreed to leave with him.'

'And you used his share of the proceeds of the robbery to buy The Gemstone hotel,' Luke said.

'Some of it, yes,' Faith said. 'I did that before Jeremy could squander it away on liquor and women. But after he died, I used the rest of the money help two or three other people in town start their businesses. Gus Tute and Pete Buss, for instance.' She looked at Luke. 'Have you told Sheriff Yapp that Jeremy. . . ?'

'Nope,' Luke said. 'I ain't said nothin'.' His features softened. 'Don't plan to, now I've heard your side of the story.'

She put a hand on his arm. 'It's more than I deserve,' she said. Her face coloured slightly. 'What are your plans? Are you . . . are you going to stay in Jeopardy?'

He nodded. 'At least until Carrie is on her feet again,' he said. 'Then . . . well, if there's a reason for stayin'. . . .'

'I-I hope you can find a reason, Luke,' Faith said, dropping her head and avoiding his eye.

He stretched out a hand and lifted her chin. 'Me, too,' he said. 'Me, too.'